Whispers of Nantucket

The Coleman Series

Katie Winters

Chapter One

October 1982

It was another stormy night on Martha's Vineyard. From where he lay in bed next to his wife, Mia, Chuck Coleman watched through the crack in the drapes as lightning burst through a jet-black sky. Waves surged against the stones that lined the beachside property. October was rife with this kind of weather on the Atlantic; he'd always known this because the ocean had raised him. He knew it as well as his own body—sometimes even better.

However, the difference between this October and all those previous ones was that Chuck Coleman was on Martha's Vineyard. After years of living two separate lives, a life of lies and confusion, he'd left Nantucket—and his first family—for good. And for whatever reason, maybe it was his imagination or his guilty conscience, he felt as though these October storms on Martha's Vineyard were a thousand times more harrowing, as though God himself was prepared to rip Martha's Vineyard out of the ocean and throw it through the sky. Maybe Chuck deserved it. But all of Martha's Vineyard certainly didn't. His girls and new wife certainly didn't.

The attempt to sleep was useless. Chuck knew better than to try. It felt like a waste of time.

Carefully, so as not to wake his wife, Chuck got out of bed and tiptoed to the hallway, where he closed the door behind him and then opened Meghan's and Oriana's bedroom doors to check on them. Look at how tender they looked! How sweet! But time was passing too quickly. Oriana was already ten, and Meghan was seven years old. His heart swelled with affection for his little girls. Although he loved his second wife, Mia, dearly—with his entire heart—it wasn't lost on him that he'd finally gotten up the nerve to go to Martha's Vineyard for good because he wanted to help raise his little girls. Roland and Grant were both fully grown now. Plus, they hated him for what he'd done.

Chuck would have liked to shield them from that reality as long as he could. But they'd found out about his affair and second life on their own. And they wanted nothing to do with him anymore. Well, they wanted everything to do with his money, but that was something else. It couldn't be helped. Maybe Chuck had raised his boys to be selfish and money-driven. Perhaps that was to be expected since he'd been selfish and money-driven for much of his own life.

Children always paid attention.

Chuck wandered downstairs and made himself a mug of tea. Rain splattered the back patio and glinted on the window. The clock over the stove said it was just past eleven thirty, which meant there was still hope for him. If he got to bed by one or two, he'd still be able to work tomorrow.

Chuck went to his study to read for a little while. He was in the middle of *Moby Dick*, a novel about a madman's quest to kill a big white whale. It hadn't taken Chuck long to see himself as the main character. Maybe his quest for happiness was akin to the main character's quest to kill Moby Dick. Perhaps that was why he'd cheated on Margaret. Maybe life was a continual battle—a long, difficult journey punctuated by moments of joy. The births of his four children—each of them, including Roland and Grant—had been sensational moments for him. Sometimes he wished he could have bottled his emotions when he'd held each of them for the first time. He would have liked to return to that feeling every once in a while, the way you could return to a photograph or a favorite meal. But babies grew up quickly. Memories became foggy.

The storm petered out by midnight. Still, Chuck wasn't sleepy. He imagined that the minute he slipped into bed next to Mia, he'd toss and turn, his thoughts spinning with anxiety until he was forced out again. Rather than pour himself a glass of whiskey—which he might have done back in Nantucket—he decided to go for a walk to clear his head. It was in the low fifties, warm enough for just a light jacket, and he put on a pair of rain boots and a bucket hat and stepped onto the back patio, closing the door behind him. The clouds were moving quickly over a nearly full moon, and Chuck thought that was fitting. After all, it was nearly Halloween. The girls had already picked out their costumes, and he'd promised to take them trick-or-treating, just as he'd once taken Roland and Grant.

Aren't you done with parenting? a friend from out of town had asked him when he'd told him what was happening and that he had two secret little girls who needed him. *Haven't you had enough?*

How could anyone "have enough" of this?

Parenting was one of the most soul-affirming, difficult, and remarkably beautiful things Chuck had ever done. He'd built an enormous business and made buckets of money. But he'd also taught his children to ride their bikes. He'd taught them how to tie their shoes. He'd taught and taught and taught. He just hoped they didn't learn too much from him. He hoped they never wronged their romantic partners the way he had. He hoped they were honest and genuine.

It didn't matter that Margaret had cheated on him first. He'd forced her into that, too.

Oh, Margaret. He thought of her now, imagining her the way she'd been when he'd first met her. How he'd loved her! His Nantucket Princess. They'd sailed for hours and hours, kissing beneath cerulean skies, never imagining for a second that they wouldn't be together. Never imagining that they'd fall in love with anyone else.

Chuck started walking down the beach toward the lighthouse. As ever, it flashed its big light across the land-scape and over the water, around and around. Back in Nantucket, Chuck hadn't lived near the lighthouse, and this one intrigued him so much that he found himself walking toward it as though it were his guiding light. He hadn't thought to bring a flashlight, but he had the moon and the lighthouse. What else could he ever need?

When Chuck approached the lighthouse, something caught his eye along the water. A man stood gazing out across the waves, smoking a cigarette. Chuck guessed the man was maybe ten years older than Chuck's fifty-one—in his sixties, at least—although the wind and sun and salt did something to sailors' and seamen's faces that made them look more rugged and older.

The man sensed Chuck and turned to scowl at him. Although Chuck was still on the beach, he was pretty sure he was on private property or else the portion of the beach that belonged to the lighthouse. He took a step back and waved his hand with an apology.

But the man beckoned for Chuck to come closer.

A shiver went down Chuck's spine. Without knowing why, exactly, he went over to the man. Maybe he was too curious not to. But more than that, Chuck was a man of six-foot-three with broad shoulders. Nothing much in the world scared him—save for loneliness and his children's safety.

"Evening," Chuck addressed the man, whom he didn't recognize as he approached. But that wasn't so strange. Although he'd done business on Martha's Vineyard for years and spent many weeks with Mia, Oriana, and Meghan, he hadn't properly lived here till now. It meant he didn't know everyone the way he did in Nantucket.

Meeting a stranger was a relatively new concept to him.

"Good evening." The man raised two fuzzy eyebrows.

"Chuck Coleman." Chuck extended his hand.

"Ah! The adulterer." The man pressed his lips together as his eyes shifted. They were difficult to read.

Chuck shimmered with anger. It wasn't surprising that this man had heard of him since Martha's Vineyard and Nantucket thrived on gossip. But it was a shock that he'd come out with it just like that.

He's one of these sailor types, Chuck thought. Harmless but a waste of my time.

"I'm sorry," the man said, shaking his head. "That was rude of me. I spend almost all of my time alone. It does something to the head. I'm Clarence Knight."

Chuck shook Clarence's hand but still decided to head home. "Pleasure."

Clarence tilted his head toward the lighthouse. "I work up there."

Chuck's curiosity was piqued. "You're the lighthouse keeper!"

Clarence's eyes glinted as though he knew this was the kind of thing that would impress someone like Chuck. "My son is up there right now, taking care of the light. His mother died many years ago. But he's older now and much more mature than I was at that age. He's capable of taking on the light, I reckon."

Chuck nodded, thinking of Roland and Grant, wondering if they'd ever talk to him again.

"Would you like to see it?" Clarence asked.

Chuck couldn't say no.

Clarence put out his cigarette and put it in a little box he kept in his pocket, presumably because he didn't want to litter on such a gorgeous beach, then led Chuck through the rocks to the bright red door of the lighthouse. Once inside, they climbed up and up and up the stairs all the way to the top, where Clarence's son manned the light. His son was maybe sixteen or seventeen, fresh-faced and innocent in a way that contrasted his father's face remarkably. It was hard to imagine that Clarence had ever looked like that, but Chuck had seen his own father's transformation from young man to older man and knew it could be abrupt. For whatever reason, Chuck looked slightly younger than he was. Mia's theory about that was that she was forty-one and ten years younger than him, and therefore, she "kept him young." But all the heartache in his life should have aged him. Shouldn't it have?

Clarence's son, Travis, showed Chuck around the little room at the top of the lighthouse. He seemed pleased to explain the various mechanisms to Chuck, speaking animatedly. It occurred to Chuck that it was a school night. Wasn't Travis supposed to go to high school tomorrow? But he decided it was rude to ask. Maybe Travis had flunked or dropped out. Maybe Clarence had decided to homeschool him.

"It's the first time my dad ever let me operate the place by myself," Travis explained, rubbing his palms together.

"How did it go?" Chuck asked.

"He's a natural, like his father," Clarence said from behind Chuck.

Chuck turned as Clarence bent down to retrieve some whiskey from a cabinet. Chuck wondered if Clarence was using his son as a sober lighthouse keeper so he could fade in and out of tipsiness throughout the night. *When did lighthouse keepers go to bed?* Chuck wondered. Was it up to them to stay up all night to make sure the light didn't go out?

Chuck had lived on an island all his life. Why didn't he know the answer to that?

"Let me pour you a drink," Clarence offered. "You need one."

Chuck rubbed the back of his neck and thought of his

wife and daughters back home. They probably hadn't even realized he was gone.

He thought of Margaret sleeping in the bed they'd shared for years—all the way over on Nantucket. Had she seen the same storm?

He thought of the grandchildren Roland and Grant would never let him see again. Maybe they'd have children in the future, too. Maybe Chuck would never know about them.

"Yeah. I need one," Chuck admitted. His heart shattered at the edges.

In the lighthouse towering over his adopted island of Martha's Vineyard, Chuck allowed himself a few moments of reprieve. He didn't think about how much he blamed himself for everything that had gone wrong. He didn't feel the staggering weight of regret.

But then, something happened.

"Wait." Chuck hurried to the window to peer out into the black. "I think I saw something."

"Was it a sea monster?" Clarence asked with a short laugh.

Chuck didn't answer. He fixated on that spot in the far distance, waiting for the light to flash over it again.

When it did, he barked, "A ship! There's a ship!"

It was so far in the distance that it was difficult to make out. In some ways, it really did look like a massive sea monster, all tilted and strange in the black. But something was off about it. Its lights were off, for one, which maybe meant it had lost power. And two, Chuck was pretty sure too much of the bow was dipped into the water.

The storm had taken hold of it.

Clarence and Travis came to the window to follow his

gaze. When they saw what he saw, Clarence hurried to sound the alarm and call the Coast Guard. Things sped up after that. Chuck watched from the window as helicopters and boats sped out to the great sinking vessel. His heart pounded in his throat. Beside him, Travis and Clarence were quiet and solemn, neither willing to admit that Chuck had been the one to see the ship first and, therefore, do their job for them. But Chuck wasn't one to cast blame. Most likely, they would have seen the ship eventually. Probably.

Chapter Two

I t was the morning of Thanksgiving and the chilliest day of the year so far. Seventeen degrees! Estelle stood in her kitchen with a mug of hot coffee, watching as the fog rolled over the Nantucket Sound and listening as, upstairs, her husband, Roland, shifted through his early morning preparations, still groggy enough to make mistakes. He dropped things and maybe stubbed his toe. She listened to his mild cursing and cringed. But when Roland appeared in the kitchen, still wearing his big fluffy robe, his smile was enormous, and he kissed her on the lips and said, "Happy Thanksgiving, my love!"

Estelle giggled and leaned against him. She'd already begun dinner preparations, and the smell of sweet potatoes and turkey drifted from the oven. Her to-do list was about a mile long, but her daughters and daughter-in-law would be here soon to help. Plenty of other Colemans had agreed to bring side dishes and pies. As it had been since the two sides of the Coleman family had come together, Thanksgiving was going to be massive.

"I can't believe we're crazy enough to host everyone," Estelle said, reaching up to touch Roland's cheek, which was still fuzzy pre-shave.

"I'm bracing myself for a storm!" Roland joked, turning to pour himself a mug of coffee.

Estelle watched him, his broad back facing her as the coffee filled a mug her publisher had sent her a couple of years ago. Roland was the man of her dreams, the man of her heart, and the father of her three children. He was also, she knew, rather complicated, occasionally secretive, and forever nursing the broken heart he'd garnered when he'd learned about his father's affair and second family. The fact that Roland had taken so much hush money from Chuck in the wake of that discovery was something Estelle had made peace with. Roland and Grant had forgiven themselves—and one another—for being so cold-hearted. Best of all, they'd forgiven Chuck, mending a relationship they'd abandoned in the early eighties.

Chuck was in his nineties now. Estelle firmly believed that everyone deserved forgiveness, no matter what they'd done, as long as they apologized and asked for forgiveness. That was her top tip for longevity in marriages. Forgive each other. Move on. Love well every day.

Estelle's phone buzzed with a text from Samantha, their middle child. She sent a selfie with her daughters, Rachelle and Darcy, beneath the arrivals gate at the Nantucket Airport.

The text read: Look who I found!

Warmth flooded through Estelle's arms and legs. "Look, Rolly! Our girl is home!" She flashed the screen of her phone toward her husband, who raised his mug and smiled.

"Does she remember how to speak English?" he joked.

"We'll all just have to learn Italian if she forgot," Estelle said, unable to stop smiling.

Last summer, after a raucous experience with The Cooking Channel at a restaurant here in Nantucket, Rachelle was hired to work as a chef in Rome. She'd leaped at the opportunity, telling her family she'd be back "as soon as she could." Estelle hadn't believed her. She'd known that the minute she was out in the wild world of food and travel, of Italian men and nightlife, of pasta and pizza and red, red wine, Rachelle would struggle to remember how magical Nantucket really was. Maybe she'd be back one day. But not soon.

Estelle was careful never to mention this to Samantha or Darcy. Darcy was Rachelle's very best friend and slightly older sister, and prior to Rachelle's departure, they'd lived together in Nantucket's Historic District. But now, Darcy was pregnant, and time was speeding up.

Before Darcy and Rachelle knew it, they'd be in their thirties or forties, talking about "the good old days" when they'd spent a few summers together. Back before their "real lives" had begun.

Estelle was a popular romance novelist. For this reason, she sometimes felt she read all of her friends' and family members' life stories as though they were as-yet-unfinished novels. Roland sometimes accused her of this, saying, *This isn't a book, Estelle. It's real life. Nothing is ever as romantic or fantastical.*

But Estelle begged to differ. Life was full of surprises. You didn't have to be a writer to recognize that.

Estelle continued her work in the kitchen. Roland went upstairs to shower and change. Very soon, his half sisters, Oriana and Meghan, would bring their families and Chuck over from Martha's Vineyard by ferry, which operated sparingly over the holidays. As ever, when his half sisters and father were coming, Roland was jittery. It was like he couldn't fully relax into those new relationships.

But Oriana, Meghan, and Chuck had come into their lives just last year. There was a lot of love there, but comfort would take time.

Suddenly, there was a knock on the door. It was only eight fifteen, but already Samantha had brought Darcy and Rachelle over to hang out with their grandmother in the kitchen and prep, prep, prep. Estelle opened her arms to Rachelle, who looked tan, happy, and healthy. She wore clothes Estelle didn't recognize, a black dress that seemed very Italian. Estelle searched her voice for any sign of an Italian accent to her English words, frightened that it had crept in and changed her. But Rachelle was the same as ever.

"It's so good to see you, Grandma," Rachelle said.

Darcy looked even more pregnant than she had last week. Her cheeks were flushed pink, and she hugged her grandmother nearly as long as Rachelle had.

"Your sister's back!" Estelle announced to Darcy.

Despite her pregnant belly, Darcy looked as though she might float into the sky with joy.

Samantha hurried in after them, closing the door tight against the chill. "It's twelve degrees!" she cried, smiling.

"It's amazing," Rachelle said wistfully. "It never gets this cold in Rome. I've missed it."

Back in the kitchen with three of her favorite girls,

Estelle felt a new jolt of energy. Unsurprisingly, Rachelle wanted to make a few brand-new Italian recipes for dinner, and Estelle gave her space and time to work.

"When you have a professional chef in the family, you let her do what she wants!" Estelle declared, watching her granddaughter slice and dice vegetables quickly and succinctly. She looked just like the chefs on television.

"Tell me," Estelle begged as she began to make the dough for the dinner rolls. "How is Rome? What is your life like?"

Rachelle blushed and glanced at Darcy. It was clear she was weighing up how much she should tell her grandmother about her "real life." In Rachelle's eyes, Estelle knew she was about a thousand years old. More than that, to her, Estelle had only ever been in love with Roland. It was true she'd married young, that she hadn't had to date around much, if at all, during high school before falling and staying in love. But Estelle was a romance novelist, for crying out loud! She wanted to hear about the trials and tribulations of Rachelle's dating escapades in Italy!

But it wasn't as though Estelle would have told her grandmother about her dating life, either. She had to respect that.

"It's been interesting, to say the least," Rachelle offered.

"Come on. Tell her about Federico!" Darcy cried.

Rachelle shot Darcy a look that meant hush. Estelle's heart banged in her chest.

But a split second later came another knock on the door. It was only nine fifteen, far earlier than she'd told the Colemans to swing by for pre-dinner drinks. But

Estelle knew better than to trust her family to pay attention to instructions, not on such an important holiday.

Aria and Hilary came next. Hilary's fiancé and Aria's father, Marc, were coming at noon—the time Estelle had told everyone to come by—but Hilary and Aria hadn't wanted to miss out on any fun. They brought a wave of expensive-smelling perfume with their entrance, and Estelle hugged them and ushered them into the kitchen to hang out with everyone. Darcy had put music on Estelle's little speaker, which Estelle often forgot how to use. Estelle's smile was already hurting her face.

Hilary had brought along a number of wedding magazines, which she splayed across the kitchen table. Her wedding was just three months away in February, and she had just a few more last-minute decisions. "I need your opinions!" she cried.

"Yeah, right," Samantha joked. "What could we possibly help you with? You're the one with the artistic eye, Sis."

Hilary laughed and waved her hand even though this was entirely true, and she knew it. Hilary was a sought-after interior designer with Sotheby's. Recently, she'd trained Aria as her assistant although Aria also took on her own clients now. She had even been written about as "one to watch in the interior design scene."

Hilary flipped midway through the magazine, where beautiful and glossy models showed off bridesmaid dresses in soft lavenders and seafoam greens and powder blues. "We have to talk about what my bridesmaids are wearing!" Hilary gave each of them a pointed look, including Estelle, who blushed.

"I'd look ridiculous in something like that," Estelle declared.

"Not true!" Hilary cried. "Mom, let's get real. I'm in my forties; Marc's in his forties. It isn't going to be a traditional wedding. But I want all the most important women in my life to feel beautiful. I want you all to stand together in dresses that—most importantly—go together."

Estelle and Sam made eye contact over the kitchen table. Estelle continued to knead the dough for the rolls, thinking of the heinous diet she'd have to go on before Hilary's wedding. Maybe she could juice again? Perhaps she could just count carbs?

"No heavy diets, either," Hilary said as though she could read her mother's mind. "I want this wedding to be about accepting who we are right now. That's been Marc's and my mantra since the beginning of our new relationship. The past is the past. What's now is now."

"You know I'll be as big as a whale by then, right?" Darcy asked.

"What's now is now!" Hilary reaffirmed.

Everyone laughed. But Hilary's eyes glowed with affirmation. It was clear that this was what she wanted, that she was happier and more in love than she'd ever been. Estelle was pleased for her. When Hilary and Marc had broken up the first time—many years ago—Estelle had been brokenhearted. She'd wanted all of her children to have what she'd had: a solid foundation, a romantic life partner, a "normal" life. But Estelle knew now that nothing in life was "normal." Her children were proof of that.

"Let's pick some dresses!" Hilary suggested.

What could the Coleman women do but play along?

Not long after that, the rest of the tremendous Coleman family arrived. Estelle was launched into the last few hours of pre-dinner chaos, which found reason and organization only because of Rachelle's vast background in rush-hour kitchens. People milled in and out of the kitchen, hunting for bottles of wine and bottles of beer and bottles of Diet Coke. Estelle threw her arms around everyone as they passed, dotting them with flour and anything else she might have on her hands.

From the kitchen, Estelle overheard Chuck Coleman greeting everyone with his enormous, booming voice. It was remarkable that a man of ninety-three could control a room like that. But Chuck Coleman was that kind of man: passionate, open-hearted, curious, and eager.

"I'd better go say hi to Great-Grandpa," Rachelle said, washing her hands quickly and heading into the living room.

"Ciao, Bella!" Chuck greeted Rachelle with a near-perfect Italian accent. "There she is. Back from the old country!"

"Grandpa, we're not Italian!" Rachelle said.

Estelle remained in the kitchen, drying her hands and listening to the thick wave of Colemans as they talked over one another, clinked glasses of wine, and commented on how "delicious the food smelled." Her heartbeat slowed. Outside, a soft snow began to fall from the rolling gray clouds above, and she took a moment to say a prayer of thanks.

This is the happiest life I've ever known.

The Colemans sat for Thanksgiving dinner at two p.m. Like every year, Roland was given the knife to carve the turkey, and everyone passed mashed potatoes and gravy, brussels sprouts, rolls, cheesy potatoes, baked beans, salads, and a few different types of Italian pasta around the table, heaping spoonfuls on their plates. Estelle's glass of wine was full, and she raised it with everyone else as they gave thanks. Across from her sat Grandpa Chuck, who didn't drink much wine anymore but who'd put a splash of wine in his glass for toasting. His eyes glinted mischievously. It always seemed to Estelle that he had a thousand tricks up his sleeve despite his age.

The food was good. Everyone told Estelle she'd outdone herself, and Estelle insisted she hadn't, that this or that was overcooked or too salty.

"It's perfect, Estelle," Roland assured. "I wore my biggest pair of pants and am prepared to loosen my belt within the hour."

Estelle giggled and sipped her wine.

"So, Estelle," Chuck said, directing his attention toward her, "are you working on anything at the moment?"

Estelle was taken aback. It was rare that anyone asked about her writing process. But Chuck had mentioned before that he was fascinated with her career. He'd even read a few of her novels, which made her blush. The man loved romance, apparently. Maybe it shouldn't have been a surprise. After all, he'd left his first wife for a passionate affair with his second. It didn't mean he was the most loyal of men, but it did mean he had a heart.

"Estelle is always working on something," Roland announced. "She gets up way before me and goes to her office to write and write and write. Sometimes I don't even see her till late afternoon! I have to fend for myself." Roland winked to prove he was teasing.

Estelle laughed. "I get obsessed with my stories," she agreed. "But it's the only way I've ever known how to work. Real life fades away."

"It's romantic," Chuck said. "I imagine that's how most successful writers work."

Estelle realized that quite a few of the Colemans were tuning in to listen to their conversation. Even Oriana, at the far end of the table, had her head tilted with curiosity.

Estelle took a bite of mashed potatoes and smiled, thinking the conversation was over. She glanced down at the table to see that Hilary and Marc were holding hands over the table, as though they were teenagers who couldn't help it.

"But what about the content of the story?" Chuck asked eagerly. "Who are the characters? Set the scene!"

"Dad, Estelle doesn't ever talk about that." Roland laughed. "Trust me, I've tried to get details out of her for years. She keeps it all locked tight."

Estelle laughed and smiled.

"Not even a hint?" Chuck asked.

"All right." It was Thanksgiving, and Estelle felt especially loose today. "It's about a lighthouse keeper. That's all I'll say." She pretended to zip her lips and throw away the key.

Chuck's face immediately transformed. His eyes were illuminated. "A lighthouse keeper," he repeated.

"That's romantic," Samantha said from a few seats down. "Who does he fall in love with in the story, Mom?"

"I can't share anything else!" Estelle said with a secretive smile.

But Chuck continued to look contemplative. "I knew a lighthouse keeper once."

Roland perked up. "Here in Nantucket?"

Chuck shook his head. "I met him in Martha's Vineyard."

Roland looked slumped for a moment but soon

corrected his posture. Estelle knew he didn't like to be reminded of his father's departure, of his second wife, Mia, or of the painful 1980s.

But something about Chuck's expression gave Estelle pause.

"You have a story," Estelle said suddenly. "A story about this lighthouse keeper. Don't you?"

Chuck laughed, but this time, the humor didn't rise to his eyes. "It's nothing. A story from a million years ago."

It was clear he didn't want to talk about it anymore. He twisted away and looked at Rachelle. "Could you pass the cheesy potatoes, dear?" His tone was entirely different.

Estelle was taken aback. She knew the older man had secrets, just like everyone. But she'd assumed that most of their big secrets were out in the open now that both sides of the Coleman family were back together again.

What was Chuck hiding this time?

She wondered if she'd ever find out.

Chapter Three

Present Day

It was seven thirty the night of Thanksgiving, and Chuck Coleman was eating his third slice of pie. It was pumpkin, his favorite, although pecan was a close second. "I'm going to regret this," he said to Rachelle, his great-granddaughter who lived in Italy.

Rachelle laughed and told him, "Life's too short, and Thanksgiving comes around only once a year." He smiled at that. Rachelle seemed to get something about life, something that had passed him by when he was that age. Over there in Rome, she was trying to make something of herself. Chuck prayed she'd come back someday. But by then, he reckoned he wouldn't be alive anymore. He was already ninety-three years old, for crying out loud. How long could a body last?

Chuck didn't feel especially old, not in his mind, anyway. He still did the crossword every morning; he could still recall, with startling accuracy, trivia from forty, fifty, or sixty years ago. He knew all the lyrics to his favorite songs by Bob Dylan, and he could still drive although he didn't always choose to because his daughters panicked about it. He didn't like to see their faces all screwed up with worry.

Now, Chuck was in Roland's living room, seated between Rachelle and his other son, Grant. Across the room from them was Sophie, Grant's daughter and his granddaughter, who'd just given birth to his great-grand-child, who lay in her arms sweetly. The baby hadn't woken up once since just before lunch. Sophie glowed with happiness, talking quietly to her cousin Charlie, whose children were down in the basement with their cousins.

Sometimes it boggled Chuck's mind to remember that his family was back together again. It wasn't so long ago that they'd been separated by that stretch of water between Nantucket and Martha's Vineyard. It wasn't so long ago that he'd thought Grant and Roland would never talk to him again.

Here they were together, so many of the Colemans under one roof. They were the result of his love for Margaret and his love for Mia. The result of his love and his betrayal. But nobody seemed to care much about what he'd done anymore. His reasoning was that people couldn't hate a man as old as him. He probably seemed so weak and incapable.

Roland's wife, Estelle—the romance writer—breezed in and out of the living room, fetching fresh glasses of wine and cans of beer. She had the air of someone with unlimited energy. She was in her late sixties, still bright and snappy and creative.

She was writing a story about a lighthouse keeper. But that was all she wanted to say.

She's secretive. Like me, Chuck thought.

Chuck had, of course, met Estelle when she was a high school student and Roland's girlfriend. But at the time, Chuck had been up to his ears in the horrors and complications of raising two families at once. He hadn't had much time to get to know Estelle, not that Estelle or Roland had necessarily wanted to hang around him back then. But it was strange to get to know Estelle now as an "older woman," a woman who'd stood by his son through thick and thin. What had she thought about Roland taking the hush money from Chuck? Did they still talk about it? Or had that story been buried by a thousand others? That was the way of marriage, Chuck knew. You had to pick your battles. You had to learn to forgive and move on.

Right now, Grant and his wife, Katrina, recalled the night Sophie gave birth.

"It was two in the morning when we got the call, right, Katrina?" Grant turned to his wife, his eyes alight. "Katrina got out of bed like it was on fire. I didn't even know she already had a bag packed!"

Katrina laughed. "When your daughter needs you, you have to be ready."

To her right, Samantha nodded. Chuck thought she was mentally taking notes since her daughter, Darcy, would be having a baby soon. Darcy's fiancé, Steven, was around here somewhere. Chuck didn't know him well, but he seemed like an earnest and big-hearted islander. What more could Darcy want?

Even more weddings and babies and celebrations lurked on the horizon. Chuck prayed he would be around for many, many more of them.

Someone touched his shoulder from above. Chuck

turned his head to see Oriana, his eldest daughter, smiling down at him. "You feeling okay, Dad?"

Chuck wanted to roll his eyes. Oriana was always on his case about his health, how tired he was, and whether or not he needed a nap or a sandwich. He'd literally raised her. Didn't she remember? But she was a high-powered art dealer with a control freak problem. Everyone who loved her knew that much about her. They all had to deal with her constant worries and big, big heart.

Chuck had always been a control freak, too. She came by it honestly.

"I feel fantastic," Chuck said. "And you?"

"I feel like I ate a truck." Oriana laughed, squeezing his shoulder again. "You'll let me know if you need anything?"

"Will do." Chuck winked, hoping his playfulness would get her off his back.

The plan was for Chuck to spend the night at Roland and Estelle's tonight and take the ferry back to Martha's Vineyard tomorrow morning. Oriana's and Meghan's families had booked hotel rooms in the Historic District, but Chuck was welcome with his eldest son. Chuck's stomach twisted with nerves. Sometimes he pictured the night ahead with joy: him and Roland and maybe even Grant, staying up to watch a documentary or a film. Other times, he was fearful and pictured it like this: Roland saying something snide about Chuck having left his first wife, and Chuck saying something awful that he would regret later.

We're older now. We know how to forgive, he reminded himself.

By eight, the Colemans had begun to filter out of the house, holding their stomachs and thanking Estelle. Their eyes were small and tired. Chuck got up to hug a few of them until his knees protested. He stayed on the sofa, taking people's hands and squeezing them.

Oriana kissed Chuck good night and said, "We'll be here in the morning to pick you up! Eight?"

"I'll be ready," he promised. It would be easy for him. He always got up at six thirty, no matter what. It was a habit left over from his working days and his days of child-rearing. He couldn't shake it.

Life began at six thirty. If he slept in, he missed it.

Not so long after that, it was only Chuck, Roland, Estelle, Grant, and Katrina in the living room of Roland's house. It was nearly nine thirty, but Chuck didn't feel tired.

From where they sat, they listened to the dishwasher work overtime.

"Thank goodness for that thing," Estelle said happily. "Rachelle, Sam, Hilary, and Aria scrubbed the rest of the dishes, and my kitchen is already sparkling clean!"

"It means you can get back to work bright and early tomorrow?" Chuck asked.

Estelle made a face. "I'll still be groggy from food tomorrow, I guess."

"And it's Black Friday!" Katrina reminded her.

Estelle snapped her fingers. "That's right. You still want to check out the sales downtown?"

"I'm ready!" Katrina cried.

"Any chance we swing by to see the baby afterward?" Estelle asked. "I can't get enough of that little face!"

"Sophie says I'm welcome whenever I want to visit," Katrina said. "She likes to put me in charge so she can get things done around the house and nap. But I love every second!"

Estelle puffed out her cheeks. "I can't believe how long it's been since I was a new grandmother. I still remember holding all of them in my arms." She held her arms out loosely as though in mourning for the time that had already passed by.

Chuck wanted to tell her there was still so much to look forward to. But he felt quiet and strange, lost in the fact that he'd missed watching his Nantucket grandchildren grow up. He'd been one island over as they'd celebrated birthdays, won soccer games, and learned to play instruments. He'd been so close that the Martha's Vineyard lighthouse shone its searchlight on Nantucket every night.

Roland got up to look for the remote so they could watch television. Grant and Katrina gathered their things together, yawning as they said goodbye. This left Estelle and Chuck still planted on their cushioned chairs.

Chuck felt Estelle's eyes upon him. They burned with curiosity.

"You know," she said, "I wouldn't mind hearing your story of the lighthouse keeper. I'm still in the research phase for my new novel, and it sounds like you might be the perfect person to talk to."

Chuck turned to look at her. He was surprised she was digging deeper. Hadn't he made it clear he didn't want to talk about it?

Roland returned with the remote control and sat back down. "What about a Christmas film?"

Chuck wrinkled his nose. "I don't know about that. Nothing too cheesy. I know I'm a great-grandfather and a million years old, but I like good stories. I like good acting. I like good cinematography."

"That's right," Estelle remembered. "You're in the film club back in Martha's Vineyard."

That wasn't all. Chuck had actually founded the film club at his retirement facility. Every week, they watched internationally recognized, prestigious films. Films that had won Oscars and gotten standing ovations at the Cannes Film Festival.

Roland laughed openly. "Let's look for something else, then. Something good enough for Chuck Coleman." He winked.

Estelle left and returned with refills of wine for herself and Roland and a mug of tea for Chuck. Chuck thanked her and settled in, grateful Roland had selected a film from Martin Scorsese. In Chuck's mind, he was one of the greatest directors who'd ever lived.

Outside, the snow swirled through the darkness, capping the island in white.

The following morning, Chuck woke up at six thirty and padded downstairs to find Roland and Estelle already up with mugs of coffee and slices of toast with butter. Estelle greeted him happily, but the strange glint in her eyes proved she hadn't forgotten his comment about the lighthouse keeper.

When will you learn to keep your big, fat mouth shut, Chuck? he asked himself. *You're ninety-three years old, for crying out loud!*

Chuck enjoyed a small breakfast with Roland and Estelle before Oriana and her husband, Reese, came to pick him up. The rest of their side of the family—the Mia side—had already driven to the ferry and were waiting on them. Chuck hugged Roland and Estelle goodbye and got into the front seat of Reese's car, buckling himself in as Oriana said a final goodbye.

"You must be tired, Dad," Oriana suggested from the back as they drove.

Chuck refused to admit he was tired. "I feel great."

On the ferry, Chuck kept the ruse going. He sat at a table with his granddaughter Alexis—the painter—and her son, Benny, who'd recovered from a horrific bout of cancer just last year and was now the bounciest, happiest little boy ever. From where Chuck sat, he could keep tabs on Alexis's brother Joel and his family, who'd recently moved back to Martha's Vineyard after years away. Joel and Reese now owned a company together and were getting closer, recovering from past wounds, just like Chuck, Roland, and Grant.

"We thought we'd grab brunch and go shopping in Oak Bluffs when we get back," Meghan suggested, walking by Chuck's table. "What do you think?"

Chuck didn't want his family time to end. "Count me in!" He could sleep later.

From the Oak Bluffs harbor, Chuck could just barely make out the tip of the old lighthouse, which no longer required an operator, not now that everything was automatic. Alexis informed him that plenty of lighthouses were now being offered "for free" to people who wanted to maintain their beauty. Apparently, you could fill out an online application.

Where were Clarence and Travis now? Chuck hadn't heard mention of them in years. How had they gotten into the lighthouse-keeping business in the first place? He'd never thought to ask.

They milled through Oak Bluffs for a little while, popping in and out of stores to check out the Black Friday sales. But the air was still frigid—barely twenty-five degrees—and Meghan eventually convinced Oriana to duck into their favorite brunch place for a while. Chuck was frozen, rubbing his hands together to warm up. But the vibrant and happy brunch spot was filled with people he'd known since the eighties and nineties. He spotted Wes Sheridan and his new bride, Beatrice, in the corner, enjoying heaps of pancakes and an omelet to share. Wes got up to shake his hand.

"There he is!" Wes said.

Chuck was quite a bit older than Wes Sheridan, and in Wes's eyes, he still saw the respect he'd garnered over the years from younger men. In Wes's eyes, Chuck was still a prosperous businessman and an important member of the community in Martha's Vineyard. Everyone knew Chuck had come to Martha's Vineyard to be with his second wife, but Wes, especially, didn't judge him for that. His life had been messy, too. His wife, Anna, had been cheating on him the night she'd drowned.

It was a horrible story. But Wes had recovered, mostly, as had his three daughters, Susan, Christine, and Lola.

Chuck ordered an egg white omelet, thinking of his cholesterol, plus a biscuit because he still took pleasure in things. He'd already had enough coffee and opted for tea.

He felt Oriana's eyes on him from across the table. Should he tell her to lay off? Or would that come off as cruel?

"It's incredible to have everyone back together again, isn't it?" Oriana said.

"It's hard to believe," Chuck agreed. Suddenly, he yawned, betraying himself. He placed his hand over his mouth quickly, trying to conceal his fatigue, but it was too late; Oriana knew.

"We'd better get you back home." Oriana scrunched up her face.

Chuck sighed and stared down at his biscuit. His shoulders ached.

Not for the first time, he thought how cruel it was that he seemed to fall deeper and deeper in love with life as he got older and time slipped away. He supposed that was always the way it went.

Not long after that, Oriana and Meghan walked him into the retirement facility. The woman at the front desk —Rhonda—greeted him with a smile and bobbed her head in a way that made her Santa hat bounce. Chuck laughed. "That's some hat, Rhonda," he said. Sometimes he really resented that younger people regarded older people like him as more like children than adults. Other times, he took pleasure in the fact that getting older meant no longer caring what anyone thought. It meant taking pleasure in silly things.

Mia had been especially good at that, and he remembered now as they strolled the halls and headed for his little apartment. She'd been big-hearted and quick to laugh, always dancing in the kitchen with the girls and playing the radio a little too loud. She'd been such a contrast to Margaret. Maybe that was why he'd fallen in love with her.

Suddenly, another memory pinged from the back alleys of his mind. Mia. The lighthouse keeper. The sinking ship. Chuck stalled in the hallway and took the handrail to steady himself.

"Dad?" Oriana sounded stricken. She touched his back. "Should we call someone?"

"I'm fine, Oriana," Chuck groaned although he felt desperate and discombobulated. He wanted to sit alone in his chair and read a nonfiction book that had nothing to do with him or his personal history.

"Just tired?" Meghan asked sweetly.

Chuck didn't answer. He proceeded through the halls and turned into his room. His knees popped as he fell into his chair and adjusted himself. Oriana and Meghan hurried to make him a mug of tea and put some snacks on the table next to him.

His daughters doted on him. His heart swelled with the immensity of their love.

But he couldn't wait for them to go.

He needed to focus. He had to reject memories of the past. He had to live in the now.

The past was always apt to destroy you. He was certainly old enough to know that.

Chapter Four

At two p.m. on Black Friday, Estelle's agent called with the news. "Are you sitting down?" Christie asked, her voice sparkling with excitement.

Estelle wasn't. She stood on the driveway outside her house as a sharp oceanic wind blasted through her, rippling her coat. It wasn't terribly nice to be outside, not even for a brisk walk, but standing in the living room window, she'd noticed something wrong with the mailbox. It had tipped over in the wind, and she'd come outside to stab it back in its hole again. It hadn't sat right since last summer when some teenagers had hit it with a baseball bat. Roland commented that the more things changed, the more they stayed the same. Estelle joked that she thought teenagers had video games now! Why did they need vandalism to pass the time?

They were too old to let something so silly bother them.

"Just come out with it!" Estelle begged her agent.

"All right. Well, we just sold the international film

rights for *Forever Walk with Me!*" she cried. "Get ready for the next phase of your celebrity career!"

Estelle's eyes widened with shock. "The rights sold on the day after Thanksgiving?"

"A production company in Paris bought them," Christie explained. "They don't have Thanksgiving over there. No holiday weekend."

"Oh yes. Of course!" Estelle laughed as tears spilled from her eyes. Whenever she got good career-related news, she cried, no matter what. No matter how often it happened now. She never imagined she'd make it this far in her writing career. She never imagined people would care about what she had to say.

Estelle hurried back inside so the tears wouldn't freeze on her face. Her agent continued to tell her what had happened, how the bidding had gone, and how much the Parisian production company had paid to secure the rights. "Who knows when they'll start filming," Christie said flippantly. "These things move as slow as molasses."

"I'm not young anymore," Estelle said with a laugh. "But I'm patient."

Estelle was at the counter, buzzing with adrenaline. Not for the first time that week, she thought, *I found the perfect career. I'm living the life of my dreams.*

"Tell me about your new book!" her agent said now, her voice still chipper. "You said it was top secret, but I can't wait anymore."

Estelle winced. "I'm still in the heavy research phase."

"Does that mean you have to keep it a secret from your agent?" Christie asked.

"I'm terrified you won't like it," Estelle offered.

"When have I not liked your work?" Christie asked.

"You've vetoed plenty of ideas over the years. You vetoed the romance at the Antarctic research center," Estelle reminded her.

"Come on, Estelle. It sounded too scientific," Christie teased. "Neither of us knows anything about science!"

"You vetoed the basketball romance set in France," Estelle said.

"Since when do our readers like sports?" Christie sighed.

Estelle giggled.

"You know that I only make decisions based on what I think will work best," Christie said, sounding disappointed. "I hope I haven't hurt your feelings."

"I know." Estelle waved her hand even though her agent couldn't see her from where she sat in New York City. "I promise I'll have more information about my new book soon. After that, feel free to break my heart and veto away!"

Christie laughed. "You're the best, Estelle. You really are."

"Am I your favorite client?" Estelle teased, knowing that her agent couldn't possibly play favorites.

"All of my clients are my favorite clients," Christie said. "Don't make me choose between you all!"

Estelle got off the phone and headed to the workout room to announce the international film rights sale to Roland. Roland was on the Peloton, watching a documentary about communism, gripping the bike handles as he huffed and puffed. Estelle waited till he slowed down to tell him. When she did, he bounded off the bike and hurried over to give her a big hug and kiss.

"You're sensational, Estelle Coleman," he said. "I love you to pieces, you know that?"

Estelle floated back through the house to get ready to meet Katrina downtown. Katrina had a list of to-dos, Black Friday sales to check out, and baby supplies to pick up for Sophie, but Estelle didn't have much to do or much to buy. She would just enjoy herself, she decided. She'd celebrate in her own way.

Estelle grabbed the very last parking spot in the lot near the courthouse and hurried through the crowded sidewalks to The French Spot, a little coffee shop with brunch offerings and plenty of cakes. Katrina was already in the corner, jotting notes in a notebook Estelle remembered as Katrina's most essential accessory. She never went anywhere without it.

Katrina got up to hug Estelle. Estelle gripped her friend and sister-in-law's shoulders and said, "My book sold international film rights! In Paris, of all places!"

Katrina's jaw dropped. "You're kidding!"

Estelle sat across from her and squeezed her knees with joy. The skin on her face felt frozen, and she stretched her smile wider to warm up. The coffee shop was packed with holiday shoppers, many of whom Estelle had known all her life. A few milled past, asking Estelle about her upcoming book releases and Katrina, of course, about the new baby.

"I'm a celebrity like you!" Katrina joked to Estelle. "I forgot that a new baby brings that kind of magic to the world."

"Let's go to the baby store!" Estelle suggested. "I want to look at those little outfits and get Sophie something special and warm. Goodness, I was so nervous when I had my babies. Nantucket winters felt especially brutal."

Katrina nodded. "I remember."

It was true that they'd gone through their own era of

babies and baby raising and conceiving at similar times. But Estelle and Katrina hadn't been as close back then. Grant and Roland had been angry—both with one another and at their father—and they'd kept a healthy distance, especially after Grant followed in his father's footsteps career-wise, and Roland decided to do his own thing.

Estelle wished she and Katrina had been there for each other more often during those difficult and lonely years.

As though she could read her mind, Katrina squeezed Estelle's hand over the table. "I don't want Sophie to spend entire days alone like I did."

"No! I wouldn't wish that loneliness on anyone," Estelle agreed. She hadn't even had time to write a few words back then, let alone entire books. Becoming a novelist felt like the furthest away of dreams. "What about Patrick?"

"He took some time off to help with the baby," Katrina said. "Times are different than they were when we were young mothers. It's more accepted—and desired—that fathers are there for the infant stage. It's still hard for me to wrap my mind around it." She smiled meekly. "I hate how old-fashioned I sound, even to myself. But the truth is, I'm pleased for Patrick and Sophie. Patrick has learned so many things about taking care of a baby that Grant never did. I'm not sure Grant ever really knew what I was up to—all the sleep regression and sicknesses and endless fears and so on."

"Roland didn't know, either," Estelle said.

The two women held a moment of silence.

"Do you think Roland and Grant were even more involved than Chuck?" Katrina asked.

Estelle winced. "It's difficult to say."

"Chuck was able to have two families at once, I suppose," Katrina said with a shrug. "You hear about men doing that all the time. Never mothers."

"Never mothers," Estelle agreed.

Again, Estelle remembered Chuck's cryptic comments about the lighthouse keeper he'd once known. She was reminded that he was ninety-three years old. He probably carried a wealth of secrets within him. As a novelist, she was fascinated with that and eager to tap into that knowledge. But as his daughter-in-law, she was wary.

Estelle and Katrina had a light brunch and walked downtown, window-shopping and occasionally popping into shops to look at books, ornate pillowcases, bottles of natural wine, and adorable and pint-sized outfits for Sophie's baby. But their toes were frigid within the hour, so Katrina suggested they head to Sophie's to drop off the baby clothes and warm up.

Estelle followed Katrina's car and parked it in Sophie's driveway. As she cut the engine, she remembered the Solstice Party from just a year and a half ago, when news of Sophie's affair with Patrick had spilled out into the open. Sophie and Patrick were both addicts, hiding themselves and their drug use from their prominent families. Sophie's unhappy marriage came to an abrupt and necessary end, and she and Patrick immediately went to rehab and struck out on a journey of self-discovery and sobriety together. Already, they had a new baby. Life came at you fast.

Estelle thought it was a story that might have fit in a novel. But she would never have used Sophie's real life for inspiration like that. It felt too invasive.

Patrick opened the door for them in a pair of jeans

and a gray shirt that advertised a band Estelle had never heard of. His smile was goofy and exhausted. "Come in!" he whispered happily. "The baby just fell asleep."

Estelle and Katrina tiptoed into the living room just as Sophie tiptoed downstairs. She was wearing a big university sweatshirt and a pair of leggings with her hair in a messy bun. The baby weight probably wasn't going to budge quickly, not on Sophie's forty-something-year-old body, but Estelle had a hunch that Sophie didn't mind. Patrick didn't seem to care, either.

Estelle had felt tremendous pressure to lose the baby weight after all three of her pregnancies. Had that been self-created pressure? Societal pressure? She couldn't remember Roland saying a single thing about it.

Sophie hugged her mother and Estelle and hurried to put a kettle on the stove. Patrick shuffled to the cabinet to find snacks—a package of cookies and some crackers, which Estelle and Katrina insisted they didn't need but still nibbled on because why not?

Estelle and Katrina showed the new parents all the baby clothes they'd bought, splaying them across the sofa as Sophie watched with big eyes.

"Oh, you shouldn't have!" Sophie gushed. "But thank you."

"It's your first baby, Sophie!" Estelle reminded her. "Of course, we're going to go overboard. That's what mothers and aunts are supposed to do!"

Sophie beamed.

The baby woke up again not long after. Estelle didn't mind. As soon as she quieted down a little bit, Estelle was allowed to hold her, and the baby wrapped her hand around one of Estelle's fingers. Estelle's heart ballooned.

She reminded herself to capture this specific emotion

in her writing. The emotion of holding an innocent baby so soon after its birth.

Sophie snapped her fingers. "I overheard you talking to Grandpa about a lighthouse keeper?"

Estelle brightened and raised her chin. The baby's eyes were already closing, but Estelle still carried her.

"That's right," Katrina said. "There's a lighthouse keeper in your new book?"

Estelle laughed at herself. She'd really created intrigue around this book already. "I'm still in the research phase, to be honest. My agent might veto the idea." She raised her shoulders.

Patrick brightened. "How are you going to research?"

Estelle hesitated, not sure how much she wanted to say. "I'll probably dip into libraries in both Nantucket and Martha's Vineyard to get a better sense of how it was to live in a lighthouse. I want the book to take place between both of the islands over a number of decades. It's a story about..." She paused as the baby squirmed in her arms. "It's a story about long-lost lovers who come together after years apart."

That was pretty generic, wasn't it? It didn't give the story away.

"I'm a romance novelist, after all," Estelle said with a soft laugh. "I can't resist long-lost love!"

Everyone laughed quietly so as not to disturb the baby.

Patrick snapped his fingers. "I know a documentarian on Martha's Vineyard. He made an entire film about lighthouses around here."

Estelle raised her chin and looked at Patrick with surprise. "Really?"

For whatever reason, she'd never imagined Patrick

had this whole other side to him. She'd discredited him, which wasn't like her. She was a novelist, so it was up to her to see all sides of people. She'd failed.

She made a mental note to get to know Patrick better. She had time.

"I can give you his number," Patrick offered, rifling through things on the end table to find his phone. "He's really intelligent. I don't think he's ever forgotten a fact."

"What's his name?" Estelle asked.

"His name is Henry," Patrick said, still looking for Henry's number on his phone. "He's married to Janine? She works at the Katama Lodge and Wellness Spa. I did some work for them a few years back."

Together with his two brothers, Patrick was a handyman and a carpenter. He probably knew many people in the area intimately; he'd seen inside their houses, and he'd done their house projects for them. Each job was likely a window into another family's world.

"I've always wanted to go to the Katama Lodge and Wellness Spa!" Estelle declared. "Maybe it's finally time."

Patrick beamed and turned his screen around so she could see Henry's number. "Want me to call him? I can set up a meeting!"

"Any day next week works for me," Estelle said happily. "Thank you."

Patrick hurried off to set up the meeting, leaving Estelle with his warm, sleeping baby, surrounded by Sophie and Katrina's happy smiles.

"I guess I'm off on a research adventure!" Estelle said.

"You've got a mind of your own, Estelle Coleman," Katrina said.

Just as he'd said he would, Patrick set up a meeting for

the following Tuesday afternoon. Henry agreed to meet Estelle at the Katama Lodge and Wellness Spa, where she planned to indulge in a spa treatment and then have a glass of wine in that tremendous and beautifully lit dining room with its view of Katama Bay.

"I'll spend all day at the Katama Lodge!" Estelle said to Katrina as she prepared to leave an hour or so later. "After that, I'll swing by Chuck's retirement home to say hello."

"Good idea," Katrina said. "I'm always so worried he gets lonely in there."

"I think he has plenty of friends," Estelle said, furrowing her brow. "Doesn't he?"

Katrina raised her shoulders. The question hung between them. It occurred to Estelle that she still didn't know much about Chuck's day-to-day life or the era between 1982 and 2023—the time the two families spent apart.

She was intrigued.

What if she had him all to herself? Would he open up a little bit? Would he tell her the story of the lighthouse keeper—a story that, it seemed clear, he was unwilling to give up so easily?

Chapter Five

1982

Clarence and Chuck left Travis alone at the top of the lighthouse and pounded down the circular staircase to the wet stones and sand below. The sounds of the helicopters and sirens were horrifically loud. It was like the end of the world. Chuck's blood pressure—which his doctors had warned him about —skyrocketed. He thought of his little girls, asleep in their beds at home. He thought of Mia.

Hovering at the edge of the black water, Chuck whispered to Clarence, "What kind of boat do you think it is? Who could be on it?"

"I have no idea," Clarence muttered.

It was true that it was too dark to see much at all. In just the few minutes it had taken them to exit the lighthouse, even more of the boat had sunk underwater, giving itself over to the rolling black waves. It took every ounce of Chuck's strength to keep himself from hurrying home, grabbing his sailboat, and heading out to try to help. But what could he do? He knew that a vessel like that was more apt to sink his sailboat and drown him before he could help at all.

He felt foolish. He couldn't believe that just a few hours ago, he'd been reading *Moby Dick* and imagining himself as this great and powerful boat captain. But the ocean had a mind of its own.

"Come on," Clarence barked, turning in the sand and heading through the dark.

Chuck followed him and got into the passenger side of a big red truck. Clarence cranked the ancient engine and sped them off to the harbor. They could already see from the road that some of the Coast Guard boats were headed to shore, presumably with rescued passengers aboard. Chuck understood Clarence's will to know what had happened. He craved it, too.

He wasn't sure he would ever sleep again.

Once at the harbor, Clarence and Chuck got out of the truck and hurried to the end of the dock to ask the Coast Guard, milling around in red-and-black jackets, if they could help. Ambulances awaited the arrival of the boats.

"Hang around, fellas," one of the coast guardsman ordered. "We might need you to go out there and help. Grab a jacket." He pointed at the Coast Guard truck, which was not far away.

With big red-and-black jackets on, Clarence and Chuck watched as the first of the rescue boats arrived with people they'd saved from the wrecked ship. To Chuck, the people who'd been saved looked ordinary, just like him or Mia or anyone else from Nantucket or the Vineyard, save for the fact that they were frigid and blue. They were wrapped in blankets and shivering. The post-storm temperature had dropped below freezing. A few of them had fallen into the water. Chuck's heart pounded. It was as though his body was fighting to keep him warm.

But just then, a woman in her late thirties bucked out of the ship violently, screaming so passionately that it was initially difficult to make out what she was saying.

Finally, it came to Chuck's ears. "My daughter! My daughter! Vivian! She's still out there!" Her accent was French, which made it all the more difficult to make sense of her words.

Chuck panicked. All at once, he imagined his own daughters out in that inky-black water, drowning and frozen. The woman continued to scream and cry, and Chuck hurried over to her to throw his Coast Guard jacket over her shoulders and take her in his arms. She wailed and snapped her fist against his shoulder. "My baby!" she cried. "My daughter!"

"We have to get back out there!" Chuck called to a guard.

"They probably picked her up already," he muttered. "Another boat is coming back now."

Chuck assured the woman that her daughter would be on that boat and that she would be fine. But the woman wouldn't let go of him, and she couldn't stop screaming, either. Together, they watched as the second boat came with survivors, dropping them off on the gorgeous dock of Oak Bluffs harbor. Chuck had never seen anything so tragic before. He'd never been at the sight of an accident.

The woman's cries grew more and more staggering and horrible. Her daughter wasn't on the second boat.

"I'm going to go find her!" Chuck announced to the woman.

"I'm coming with you!" she cried.

"No!" Another member of the Coast Guard hurried forward to retain her. "You're not going back out there."

Already, Chuck and Clarence boarded the boat. Its engines roared as they shot back into the night across rocky waves that seemed apt to toss them over. It was no surprise a boat had nearly sunk tonight. The water was murderous. Chuck's stomach shifted, and he thought he might throw up. "Keep it together, Chuck Coleman," he said to himself over and over.

Before long, the boat stalled near the sight of the accident. The boat was nearly completely submerged, but a number of life jackets floated around what remained of the vessel. Most didn't have anyone in them, and Chuck was terrified that the people who'd worn them hadn't put them on properly and sank instead. That was a fear he'd had with his children over the years.

He thought of that poor woman at the harbor, crying and crying out for her daughter.

Had she used her name? He searched his memory for it until he remembered. "Vivian! Are you here? Vivian?" He called her name several more times, feeling useless and stupid in the black night surrounded by actual Coast Guard personnel. He was nothing but a fake.

"We must have gotten everyone there was to get," one of the coast guardsmen suggested to another. "We can return in the morning and clean everything else up."

It was implied that he meant the other bodies they were too late for.

"Vivian!" Chuck cried out again. He felt frantic. He gripped the edge of the Coast Guard boat, his knuckles turning white.

Beside him, Clarence muttered, "It's like they say. I think it's too late."

But Chuck wanted to call out once more. He couldn't stop himself. "Vivian!"

Out of the darkness came the slightest sound—barely a whimper.

"What was that?" Chuck whispered. He flailed a hand vaguely to the left, where the sound had come from. "Go over there! Slowly, now!"

Following Chuck's guidance, the coast guardsman inched the vessel to the left. They were careful to keep a wide berth of the bigger ship, the one sinking, because it could always take them down with it.

Chuck's heart pounded in his throat.

But suddenly, he saw a flashing hand over the waves. Someone splashed wildly, at a distance from the sunken ship, as though they'd known to swim away, away, away, so as not to be taken under.

"There!" Chuck cried.

There was no telling if it was Vivian or not. But it was someone, and that was all that mattered.

The coast guardsman crept closer as the person flailed and fought the waves. It seemed they were too exhausted to make another noise. Chuck had to restrain himself from jumping into the water to save them. When they got close enough, the coast guardsman was able to throw a rope, which the survivor took and clung onto hard. As they pulled them to a ladder up the side of the boat, Chuck could make out more of the survivor's features. Clearly, she was a young woman, maybe a teenager, with black hair and a soft face that reminded him of his Oriana and Meghan. Tears filled his eyes. He was too frightened to call Vivian's name again. If it wasn't her, it was someone else, someone necessary, someone who deserved to remain alive.

But when the woman climbed the ladder and into the arms of the coast guardsman, they hauled her out, and she spoke with a French accent, using the only words she seemed to know. "Merci, thank, oh, merci!" They draped her on a cushioned chair and threw blankets over her as she wept and shivered. The boat rocked this way and that, and Chuck nearly fell over.

Clarence was the one who eventually approached her, bowed his head kindly, and asked, "What's your name, honey?"

It took a moment for the young woman to understand. But finally, she said, "I'm Vivian."

Chuck's heart rocketed with joy.

Chuck, Clarence, and the rest of the coast guardsmen were overjoyed that they'd found another survivor in the wreckage and decided to do several more rounds to see if they'd missed anyone. But despite their tireless search, they found no one else.

Another of the coast guardsmen had helped Vivian as much as he could. He'd gotten her warm clothes from below deck, made her hot tea, and given her a snack. She was going to survive, but she couldn't stop crying. Chuck wondered if she was worried about her mother.

As they returned to the harbor, sunlight peeked over waves that seemed eerily calm after the storm and the wreckage. Chuck crept over to her and bent down to say, "Your mother is waiting for you."

Vivian's eyes were slits. It was clear she didn't understand.

That was when another member of the Coast Guard came up with a first-aid kit. "She hit her head," he explained, pointing at a gash just above her ear. Chuck hadn't seen it because her hair and the night had camouflaged it. But it was true that she was losing a lot of blood.

"I don't think she felt it at first," the guardsman said, searching through the first-aid kit for something to stop the bleeding. "I think she's a little woozy. Look at her eyes."

It bothered Chuck that he spoke about Vivian like she wasn't here. But Vivian's pupils were enormous, and she didn't speak very good English. She clutched her blanket tightly and continued to shake.

"She must have hit her head when the boat sank. We'll take her to the hospital immediately," the coast guardsman explained.

The boat purred up to the dock. Vivian's mother was sobbing at the far end, near the truck where Clarence and Chuck had gotten their jackets. Chuck wished he could speak better French. He knew a little from high school, but that was it.

The guardsmen helped Vivian onto a stretcher. Chuck pulled a blanket over her and said a few words he thought were kind and comforting in French. He then followed the stretcher down the steps to the dock.

Vivian's mother bolted forward. She looked as frantic and angry as a lion. In French, she called Vivian's name and said a million other things that Chuck couldn't understand. By then, Vivian had lost consciousness, and her mother was sobbing louder than ever.

Chuck hurried toward the woman. He wanted to explain that she would be all right.

But before he could, another member of the Coast Guard—one who'd been on the boat with them—hurried up to talk to the mother. He poked a finger into Chuck's chest and said to her, "He found your daughter. He was the one." He poked three more times and wagged his eyebrows as though this could translate anything.

But Vivian's mother seemed to get the hint—that Chuck had called Vivian's name, that Chuck had searched harder than everyone because he'd known who he was looking for.

Immediately, Vivian's mother threw her arms around him and sobbed and sobbed. "Thank you," she said in English. "Oh, thank God for you."

Chapter Six

Present Day

Friday night and Saturday were the same for Chuck. He was exhausted but didn't want to admit it. Saturday night was his friend Dan's birthday celebration in the retirement facility's main dining hall, and Chuck could only stay for a half hour before he headed back to his room to rest. A few minutes after he collapsed in his chair, there was a knock on the door. Bethany, the eighty-three-year-old woman who'd been good friends with Mia many years ago when their girls had gone to school together, poked her head in to check on him. "Are you feeling all right, Chuck? Should I call Oriana?"

Chuck blushed and forced himself to smile. "I'm just old, Bethany," he reminded her.

Bethany slipped the rest of the way through the door and wrung her hands. Chuck wasn't entirely clear on what had led her to move into the retirement facility; she was of good health and probably had many years ahead of her. Why didn't she want to live at home anymore? Chuck's only guess was that she'd gotten lonely without her husband around. He'd died a couple of years ago from liver cancer. But he'd left her enough money to do whatever she wanted, and she'd decided to move in here and join their community of old folks. Chuck was glad to have her around, although she often "tattled" on his illnesses and fatigue to Oriana. She was a spy.

"Would you like me to bring you some cake?" Bethany asked.

Chuck turned down the volume on his television. He was watching a documentary on the Civil War, a topic he was well-versed in. He hoped it would put him to sleep.

"I don't need anything at all, Bethany," Chuck said. "And do me a favor, okay? Don't tell Oriana I left the party early."

Bethany looked stricken. "I would never!" This was obviously a lie, but Chuck didn't feel like calling her out. She said, "We have to watch out for each other around here, Chuck. You know that."

Chuck turned the corners of his lips up and felt a cough tremble through his lungs. He tried to swallow it, but it soon puffed out of him, and his shoulders shook. He knew he didn't look like the portrait of health.

He didn't often get sick. But when he did, it was heinous, keeping him in bed for days at a time. During the pandemic, he'd been so terrified that he hadn't seen anyone up close for many, many months, far longer than most everyone else at the retirement home. The loneliness had nearly killed him, so much so that he wasn't sure what was worse—the disease or his broken heart.

Eventually, Bethany got the hint and headed back to the birthday party. But now that he was alone, Chuck couldn't stop thinking about his cough. Maybe he'd picked something up from his family on Thanksgiving? He pictured germs in the bottom of his lungs, multiplying and threatening to kill him, and he bolted to his feet, turned off the television, and changed his clothes. He'd read somewhere that you had to keep the lungs active and the bacteria from rotting at the base of your lungs. He was no doctor, but he'd always been active. It seemed like good advice.

It was already eight thirty when Chuck reached the gym down the hall. Just as he'd suspected, its four exercise bikes, three treadmills, and hand weights were unused at such a late hour on the weekend. It occurred to him how funny it was that the retirement facility upheld weekends and days of the week. It wasn't like any of them had nine-to-five jobs anymore. They could do whatever they wanted at any time since societal expectations were no more.

Chuck turned on the television and got on an exercise bike, gripping the handles as he watched a different documentary about a different war in a different country at a different time. He was getting tired of all these war documentaries. But as he pedaled, his brain felt more and more activated, and his breathing came quick and easy. Twenty minutes later, he was tired and slick with sweat but no longer feeling bad for himself. He decided to dip into the sauna before it closed at nine thirty.

This was always his method: keep going, never stop.

A stack of fluffy towels sat on the table beside the sauna. A female employee Chuck didn't recognize was doing a crossword at the little table near the sauna. She must have been new.

"Evening!" Chuck said to her, taking a towel.

"You're exercising at a time like this?" she asked with a smile and a silly voice.

Again, Chuck had the sensation that she spoke to him as though he were a child. Not all of the people who worked here did that, but it seemed like an overwhelming majority lately. His smile faded.

"I'll just take some time in the sauna if that's okay," Chuck said.

"It's all yours," she said. "Ring the bell if you feel lightheaded."

Chuck stepped into the sauna, which wasn't as hot as he used to like it when he was a younger man. It had to do. He sat down and closed his eyes as beads of sweat popped up along his chest and arms. As he sat there in silence, it occurred to him that Oriana and Meghan were doing their best. They cared about him and wanted him to be happy and healthy for a long time. Maybe he should call them tomorrow and apologize for being "cranky" sometimes. Perhaps he should ask them to go with him to Mia's grave this week.

It felt like ages since Mia died. The thought of her final days turned Chuck's stomach. When he'd married Margaret and then Mia, he'd never imagined they'd both die so many years before him. It felt like he was the last remaining member of a club that no longer mattered.

Sometimes he tried to remember what it was like to sleep next to a woman he was in love with. He remembered the little noises they made when they were sleeping. He remembered how his heart had burst when they'd left the bed in the middle of the night—to use the bathroom, go downstairs to read, or tend to one of the children. He'd wanted them to stay.

It wasn't lost on him that he was too old to fall in love again.

It wasn't lost on him that he—Chuck Coleman, who'd famously betrayed his wife—didn't deserve to fall in love again, either.

He wasn't sure if that was a healthy thought. But it was one he lived with.

Chuck left the sauna and gave a stern smile to the woman doing the crossword, flipping a towel over his shoulder as he went. His muscles felt limber. It was nine twenty, and he decided to grab a cup of tea and a snack and head back to his room. He was feeling better than ever. Maybe he just needed a few days to himself. Perhaps he didn't have to attend every birthday party or celebration in the dining room.

He was blessed not to be lonely. He had a tremendous family and plenty of love. He knew that.

He turned the corner and spotted a woman at the far end of the hall. With her long dark hair and her glowing face, there beneath the hallway spotlight, she looked angelic and youthful. But she was seated in a wheelchair. Her eyes stared straight ahead, almost as though she couldn't see anything. What was she waiting for? Why was she alone? How old was she? Chuck felt frozen. He really wanted to approach her.

But suddenly, a nurse stepped out of a door directly behind the wheelchair. Chuck realized she was Claire, one of his favorites, not only for her happy and welcoming smile but for her sharp wit and empathy. Unlike the others, she didn't look down on him for being old. She said something to the woman in the wheelchair that Chuck couldn't hear, and then she spun the wheelchair around and headed down the hall toward him.

The woman wasn't blind, Chuck didn't think. But her eyes seemed unfocused. It was as though her brain was elsewhere. By now, Chuck realized she was quite a bit younger than he was, maybe even a good thirty years younger, although it was difficult to say. It was rare that people in their sixties came to the retirement home. It usually meant something was really wrong with their health. They didn't stay long before they went elsewhere or passed away.

Something about this woman tugged at Chuck's heartstrings. He remained rooted in his spot.

"Chuck! How are you?" Claire smiled and stopped the woman's chair in the hall to visit.

"I just took some time in the sauna," Chuck explained. "Any chance you can get them to turn that thing up?"

"No can do, Chuck." Claire laughed. "I wish I could, but they don't put me in charge of stuff like that."

Chuck snapped his fingers. "I thought it was worth a shot." He eyed the woman in the chair. "My name is Chuck. Are you new here?"

Claire continued to smile and spoke for her. "This is Mrs. Knight," she explained. "She just arrived yesterday and is still getting her bearings. She lives down the hall from you."

Chuck wondered why the woman couldn't speak for herself, but he knew better than to pry. "Welcome," he said. "I think you'll like it here. And you're in good hands with Claire. She's the best this place has."

Claire waved him off. "You flatter me. I'm just doing my job."

Chuck gave her a pointed look. "All you do here for us —for me—means a lot," he told her.

Claire bowed her head. It was rare that Chuck passed out compliments like this, but he wanted Claire to know he meant it.

"It's a pleasure to work here," Claire said, stuttering just slightly, as though it was too emotional for her. She cleared her throat. "Mrs. Knight just took some medication. I think she's about ready for bed."

"I'm about ready myself," Chuck said. "Pleasure to meet you, Mrs. Knight. I hope you'll let me know if you need anything."

Claire wheeled Mrs. Knight the rest of the way down the hall to her new suite. Chuck hung back, then followed to his own apartment, where he showered and put on a pair of warm pajamas. Instead of bothering with more documentaries about historical topics he knew down to his bones, he got into bed and stared through the darkness.

His heart thundered with sorrow for Mrs. Knight. At that age, she should still be hiking, swimming, and traveling; she should be welcoming her first grandchild. She was probably barely retired although maybe she'd never been able to work at all due to her condition. There was so little Chuck could say about her based on his brief introduction.

But something about the younger woman broke his heart. He couldn't say why.

Chapter Seven

E stelle parked her car on the ferry. It was Tuesday at one in the afternoon, and she was one of only six vehicles, proof that tourism season had fully died. Upstairs in the little coffee shop, she sat by herself with a mug of coffee and considered the others traveling around her. Besides the twentysomething behind the counter, who wore braces on her teeth and a collared sheet with the brand name of the ferry on the left corner of her chest, Estelle was the only woman. The men looked rugged, as though they'd spent too much time in the elements: wrinkled from the sun, chapped from the cold. Their hands were worn as though they'd done too much hard labor.

Estelle liked to notice these details about people. She found that they often influenced her work. Once, she'd spied an older woman on an airplane who captured her attention so much that Estelle found a way to include her in her next novel.

The people who inspired Estelle never knew it,

though. Estelle was always careful and discreet. She didn't stare.

But she made sure to write notes in the journal she took with her everywhere she went. Now, so many years after her novelist career began, she'd filled seventeen journals.

Estelle drank her coffee and accidentally caught the eye of the twentysomething woman behind the counter. The woman watched her as she cleaned the coffee machine. Estelle pulled her lips into a smile and considered the fact that Estelle was usually the only one watching. She wasn't used to being watched back.

The ferry reached Martha's Vineyard a few minutes later. Estelle pulled her car off the ferry and drove from the harbor as her phone barked instructions back to her. Unlike her husband or Grant, Estelle didn't know Martha's Vineyard like the back of her hand. It was similar to Nantucket, but it was also a separate world with separate streets and families. It was the world Chuck Coleman had fled to when his life had fallen apart.

The Katama Lodge and Wellness Spa was built with glowing wood. It looked like a massive tree house tucked in lines of birch trees. On the opposite side of the fortress was the glowing Katama Bay itself. Estelle strode inside and said hello to the receptionist, who gave her a robe, a towel, and additional instructions. Her meeting with Henry was scheduled for four thirty, which gave her time to relax, unwind, and warm up.

It was rare that Estelle gifted herself afternoons like this. She started with a few minutes in the piping-hot sauna, where her tight muscles softened, followed by a massage and acupuncture from the lodge's in-house acupuncturist, Carmella, who explained in soft tones that she, her sister, and their stepsister owned and operated the Katama Lodge together with her stepmother, Nancy. When she learned that Estelle had a meeting with Henry, she chuckled and said, "Henry's my stepsister Janine's husband. We just adore him. Oh, but you said you're a writer? You should hear the drama of Janine's first husband. He was a crazy rich and incredibly mean man from Manhattan, the heir of a fortune. He cheated on Janine with her best friend and then died not long after that."

"That's a terrible story," Estelle breathed, looking down at the needles that poked out of her, glinting in the soft light.

"But now that Janine has Henry, she has a second chance at real happiness," Carmella said, her eyes squinting as she focused on putting another needle in Estelle's upper back.

Estelle said, "It feels like everyone on Martha's Vineyard or Nantucket has a big story like that," thinking of Chuck, Roland, and their family's drama. Carmella probably knew all about that, too, although Estelle hadn't mentioned her last name or her connection with Chuck.

"It must help your writing process," Carmella said. "You should work somewhere like the Katama Lodge for inspiration. People just tell us their stories right and left. It's a place of communion, of shucking off the past in pursuit of a clean and better future."

Before Estelle left Carmella's acupuncture office, Carmella purchased three of Estelle's books from an online retailer and said, "I can't wait to dig in! I'll have you autograph them when you come back next time."

Estelle blushed and thanked her. The air shimmered with goodwill.

After a couple of hours of pampering, Estelle returned to the changing room to put back on her street clothes and prepare for Henry's arrival. She got to the dining room ten minutes before their scheduled meeting but found Henry waiting for her with a mug of tea and a notepad. He was jotting notes to himself, muttering quietly. He probably looked a lot like Estelle did when writing notes about people she saw on the ferry.

She recognized him because she'd googled him and his work that weekend. She'd been impressed with his documentaries and his numerous accolades. However, she hadn't been able to download or stream his documentary about lighthouses in New England.

"Henry?" Estelle smiled at him.

Henry got up to shake her hand warmly. He was handsome. His hair was brushed wildly behind his ears as though the Vineyard winds had tangled it up, and he'd tried to fix it badly. "It's a pleasure to meet you, Estelle," he said. "Your reputation precedes you."

Estelle laughed and sat down. She couldn't imagine Henry having read any of her romance novels; he was an intellectual and clearly uninterested in the Harlequin genre. But after she pressed him, he explained that his wife Janine had read many of Estelle's novels and parroted the plots back to him. "She's so jealous I'm meeting you today," he explained. "She had to leave this island this week for a health conference."

"Maybe we can meet another time," Estelle said with a wave of her hand. She always liked meeting her fans, especially local ones.

A server wearing linen clothes came by to take their order. Henry got another cup of tea, so Estelle followed suit. Outside, a soft snow had begun to fall from the dark gray clouds above. With the glass window, it felt as though they sat in a big snow globe.

Estelle had a big list of questions for Henry about lighthouses in the area, about what he'd learned, about what he couldn't show on the documentary, and, most specifically, about lighthouse keepers on the islands of Martha's Vineyard and Nantucket. How had they lived?

Henry spoke with his hands flat across the table between them.

"I'm sure you know the dramatic history of whaling on these islands. Nantucket led the world in whaling for one hundred years," he began. "And you must know that many ships sank around Martha's Vineyard and Nantucket. For centuries, only a few lighthouses guided the way, which left vast territories of darkness on dangerous waters. It's unclear why they didn't continue to build to keep things safer."

Estelle made notes in her journal, a shorthand that she would translate back to herself later. As she wrote, she tried to envision the lighthouse keeper in her story, living in his lighthouse, separated from society and perhaps going mad.

Soon after, Estelle got up the nerve to ask Henry why so many lighthouse keepers went insane. She hadn't decided whether the lighthouse keeper in her novel would be like that or not. But her idea was that he was slightly mad as a result of his career—and the woman who fell in love with him helped him out of his loneliness and into the metaphorical light.

The idea was that her love was the strongest light of all.

"The lighthouse keepers were isolated from society," Henry explained. "It was just them up in those towers, forced to keep the light going. If they failed, many, many people would die. It was a lot of pressure and enough to drive anyone a little crazy. Some of them got mercury poisoning. Some became obsessed with things like rat infestations or saw something out on the water that wasn't there."

"They imagined things?" Estelle asked, breathless.

"The mind plays tricks on us when we spend too much time alone," he explained. "You're a writer, which means you have a tremendous imagination. I'm sure your mind has played tricks on you, too?"

"Oh yes," Estelle said, blushing. She looked down at her journal, trying not to remember the brief jolts of insanity she'd had when her babies were very young, and she hadn't gotten enough sleep. But she didn't want to get into that now. "I imagine the lighthouse keepers couldn't sleep very much, either?"

"During the day, maybe," Henry said. "But there were so many chores to take care of. So many ways of preparing for the night. Thousands of people on the seas relied on them for safety." He sighed. "Lighthouse keepers are unsung heroes." He snapped his fingers. "You must have heard of the 1982 shipwreck? It was autumn, I think. There wouldn't have been any survivors if the lighthouse keeper hadn't spotted the boat sinking and called the Coast Guard."

"That wasn't so long ago," Estelle breathed. "Is the lighthouse keeper still around?" *Maybe she can even interview him before she goes back to Nantucket*, she thought, hopefully.

"I wasn't able to track him down," Henry said, his eyes shadowed as though it really disappointed him. "It seems he left the island. He might be dead by now. It's hard for me to admit it, but 1982 was over forty years ago."

Estelle winced and laughed. "You're right. It's hard to believe!" She jotted another note, then asked, "What's the lighthouse keeper's name? The one who spotted the shipwreck?"

"I'll have to check my notes," Henry said, touching the back of his neck. "But I believe his first name was Clarence."

"That's a nice name," Estelle said. "You don't hear it anymore."

"It's old," Henry agreed. "But babies are being named Henry again these days. Maybe Clarence will come back?"

"Maybe Estelle will, too," Estelle said, smiling.

Estelle and Henry continued talking about lighthouse keepers and the romantic ideas of long-ago Nantucket and Martha's Vineyard into the early evening. Sometimes Estelle got so swept up in the story that she imagined salt water splashing on her face. She imagined the tremendous darkness in which the lighthouse keepers lived and the hazardous waters onto which sailors adventured to pursue money and great whales.

It was important to Estelle that her stories feel as real —to her—as they could. It was only then that she could fully integrate the story into the pages of a novel.

The process could be alarmingly complex.

Estelle finished her final note at six fifteen and stood to shake Henry's hand. "It's been such a pleasure," she said. "Thank you."

Henry walked her to the foyer, where Estelle stepped into the swirling snow and hurried to her car. Her pulse was quick, and she couldn't wipe the smile from her face.

It had been a fabulous conversation. She was beginning to fill in the missing gaps of the world she wanted to create on the page.

Instead of heading directly to the ferry, Estelle drove slowly down spindly country roads back to Oak Bluffs. There, she ducked into the parking lot of Chuck's retirement facility, cut the engine, and burst through the cold to get inside, where it was warm, far warmer than she kept her house at home. It was rare that she came to the retirement facility without Roland. She removed her gloves and hat and told the receptionist who she was there to see. "He should be home!" the receptionist said, bobbing her head so that her Santa hat bounced. "Go on in and say hello."

Estelle entered the retirement facility, striding through cozy living rooms where fake fires crackled in fake fireplaces, and televisions played sports and old movies. Estelle greeted everyone as she went by and even spotted a few women reading the books she'd written.

Before leaving the living area, Estelle saw a woman who couldn't have been much older or younger than Estelle. She sat in a wheelchair pointed toward a television that played *You've Got Mail*, but it was clear from her eyes that she wasn't watching it. Estelle's heart sank. What happened to this woman? Why was she already here at her age?

The woman gave Estelle pause. What if Estelle was just a few months or years out from living in a retirement home? What if her luck was about to run out?

She shook the thought from her mind. She knew she couldn't give it power. Long ago, she'd concluded that fear of the future was a waste of time. *Whatever will be, will be*, she thought.

Estelle reached Chuck's apartment and knocked on the door. The sound of the television came from the other side, probably a documentary. Chuck was obsessed with learning new things and maintaining his knowledge.

"Come in!" Chuck sounded chipper. Estelle hadn't realized she'd been nervous about his mood, but now, she breathed a sigh of relief.

Chuck's eyes widened with surprise when she walked in. "Hello!" He got out of his chair, his bones creaking, and reached for the remote to turn off the television.

"Don't get up!" Estelle said, but it was too late. He was already coming toward her to give her a hug.

Estelle closed her eyes when she hugged him. When she'd first met him as a teenager, he'd terrified her.

"I think I mentioned I was here on the Vineyard chatting with a documentarian?" Estelle reminded him that she'd called him.

He sat back down with a nod. "That's right. Henry. How did it go?"

Estelle went three steps over to the kitchenette to put the kettle on and make some tea for them both. In the cabinet were cookies she and Roland had brought by a few weeks ago, still in their plastic wrapping. Chuck didn't normally have much of a sweet tooth, which had made his three slices of pie on Thanksgiving funny. He was obsessed with maintaining his health.

"It was great," Estelle said of her time with Henry. "He studied lighthouses around here for years and years, and he gave me a code so I can download his documentary off the internet. Maybe I can download it for you, too? I'm not sure how it works."

Chuck tilted his head. It was difficult to read his expression.

Yet again, Estelle wanted to pester him about the lighthouse keeper he'd known. Why was he being so cagey about that?

And then, Estelle had a eureka moment. She sped across the room to deliver his mug of tea and said, "Henry mentioned a shipwreck here in Martha's Vineyard. He said it happened in 1982. An old lighthouse keeper was the one to see the sinking ship and call it into the Coast Guard."

Chuck's cheek twitched. Estelle still couldn't read his expression.

"That was the year you moved to the Vineyard, wasn't it?" Estelle asked. "1982?"

Chuck sipped his tea and leaned back in his chair. Estelle had the sense that she was speaking to a child who wanted to hide something. She was reminded of Charles when he was a boy, who'd stolen all the cookies from the cookie jar and lied about it.

"You must have heard about the wreck," Estelle said. She knew she was bothering him, but she couldn't leave without some acknowledgment from him. *What is he hiding?* she wondered.

She thought Chuck Coleman was done with having secrets.

She thought everything was out in the open.

Estelle's thoughts were tangled with confusion.

"The lighthouse keeper was named Clarence, I think. At least, that's what Henry told me," Estelle said. "Did you ever meet him?"

Is Clarence the lighthouse keeper you refuse to talk about? Estelle wanted to ask.

Still, Chuck didn't say anything. He looked contemplative.

"I'd really like to track him down for an interview," Estelle said. "Do you know if he still lives on the island?"

Chuck shook his head ever so slightly. "I don't know where he went." His eyes were shadowed.

"But you knew him?" Estelle's pulse quickened. "What was his last name? Maybe I can track him down or at least figure out what happened to him."

Maybe I can model my main lighthouse keeper after Clarence, she thought. The time period was perfect. She'd already considered positioning her novel in the late seventies or early eighties; the idea was that the hero was the final generation of lighthouse keepers, carrying the torch until lighthouses operated by actual humans were obsolete. His heroine would save him from the sorrows of his family's past and the trauma of being a lonely lighthouse keeper.

All the color began to drain from Chuck's face. Estelle raised her eyebrows with alarm.

"Chuck, are you feeling all right?" She knelt beside him and kept herself from touching his forehead, as she might have one of her grandchildren. Chuck was a grown man; he deserved her respect.

But still, his health frightened her. He was ninety-three years old!

Estelle was flustered. "Do you want me to call the nurse?"

Chuck shook his head and sipped his tea. Still, he was as pale as snow.

"I'd really feel better if we called the nurse." Stepping back, she tried to brighten her voice. She didn't want Chuck to know how worried she was.

Chuck couldn't look her in the eye. "Don't waste their time. I'm just fine."

Estelle sat across from him again and wrapped her hands around her mug. She remembered how this had all begun—when Chuck had asked her about her new novel. Chuck had pried into her creative process, and now, she was trying to pry into his dramatic history. But they were both closed-off and private. Who would break first? It seemed unlikely it would be him.

Estelle searched her mind for something else to say, anything to get his mind off Clarence, the lighthouse keeper, and 1982. Eventually, she just turned the television back on, and they finished watching a documentary about German immigrants coming in droves to the United States in the 1800s. Chuck already knew everything they said in the documentary and even shared a few more details they'd left out with her.

His brain is as sharp as a tack, Estelle thought. *He'll never let me in.*

Chapter Eight

Chuck couldn't get Estelle out the door fast enough. It seemed as though there was no end to the number of questions she wanted to ask— about his health, about his past, about whether he knew about the shipwreck of 1982. Chuck had already made up his mind to pretend to fall asleep to get her out of there when she yawned, stretched her arms, and said she'd better head out. Chuck breathed a sigh of relief and said, "That's too bad. I hope you'll come back soon."

It was rare that Estelle came to the retirement facility by herself. Chuck knew she was after his stories, that she wanted to leech from him and put everything in her book. But his past was sacred. He wouldn't give her anything.

Chuck insisted on walking Estelle to the foyer to see her off. He kept his stride brisk because he wanted to prove just how spry and healthy he remained despite his age. But when they entered the living room, he spotted the young woman again—the sixty-something in a wheel-chair named Mrs. Knight—and something clicked in his brain. He nearly toppled over.

"Are you all right?" Estelle sounded frantic. She grabbed his elbow.

Chuck forced his eyes away from Mrs. Knight and swallowed several times as the room spun. He filled his lungs. "I'm fine," he breathed.

But he'd just realized something that had rocked the foundation of his world.

"Rest up!" Estelle insisted before she sped into the cold. "Love you!"

Chuck stood at the edge of the living room, wringing his hands and watching Mrs. Knight. It was clear she wasn't entirely focused on the film someone had set up for her. But she didn't look unhappy, either. Chuck wondered how many of her mental faculties remained. Would she be able to talk to him at all? Maybe that first night was a fluke; perhaps she'd been medicated and unable to speak.

Chuck approached Mrs. Knight. "Good evening," he said.

A few other people watching the film glared at him for interrupting. Chuck wanted to roll his eyes.

But Mrs. Knight didn't give any indication that she'd heard him.

Chuck stood there as curiosity ebbed and flowed through him. If he was right—and when was he ever wrong?—Mrs. Knight's return brought many questions.

But first, he had to make sure.

Chuck walked slowly around the retirement facility. He didn't want it to seem as though he was looking for her. But when he spotted Claire down a side hallway, he raised a hand in greeting, grateful it hadn't taken more than fifteen minutes to track her down. As usual, she flashed him that friendly smile. She was wearing a pink nurse's outfit.

"Evening, Chuck!" she said. "How are you?"

"Just fine," he said, smiling. "My daughter-in-law swung by to say hello. She's a dear."

"Roland's wife? Or Grant's?" Claire was well-versed in the drama of Chuck's family life, but she didn't make a big deal about it.

"Roland's," Chuck said. "She's the novelist."

Claire snapped her fingers. "I keep meaning to read one of her books! Wow. Did she tell you what she's working on right now?"

"She's a little secretive," Chuck said.

"She has to protect her creative ideas, I guess," Claire agreed.

Chuck snapped his fingers as though something had just occurred to him. "I just walked by Mrs. Knight in the living room. The younger woman you brought in a few days ago?"

Claire continued to smile. "She's just so sweet, isn't she?"

"She is! She is, indeed. But I can't shake the feeling that I know her from somewhere," Chuck said. "What is her first name?"

"Vivian," Claire said without skipping a beat.

Chuck nearly had a heart attack, but he didn't let his shock spread to his face. "Of course! Vivian. I met her years ago. She couldn't speak more than a few words of English when I first met her, if you can believe it."

Claire's smile was a little sad. "She must have been a beautiful young woman."

"She was," Chuck remembered. He blinked rapidly. He didn't want to start crying.

Suddenly, he could hear himself—deep in the past, out on the dark water, crying and crying Vivian's name. Vivian! And there she'd been, thrashing in the waves, nearly drowned.

"Are you all right, Chuck?" Claire asked timidly.

"I'm just fine," Chuck said. He searched his mind for a lie. And then he asked, "Does Mrs. Knight have any family in the area? Who brought her in?"

He didn't normally pry like this. He hoped Claire wouldn't be alarmed.

Claire pressed her lips together. "I can't really share private details about her family," she said after a pause. "I'm sorry, Chuck."

Chuck spread his hands out in front of him. "Not a problem at all, Claire! I'm sorry for prying."

He felt foolish.

"It's possible she'll be able to speak a little bit more, sooner rather than later," Claire said. "The doctors are doing numerous tests. She's still partially there—somewhere back there."

Chuck's heart thudded. "That's good to hear," he said although he didn't let himself hope for more.

Claire said she had to head off to tend to another patient. Chuck thanked her and moseyed back toward the living room, where he stood in the corner, looking at Vivian Knight. It was hard to believe it'd been more than forty-two years since the fateful night when she'd nearly drowned. She'd been seventeen. It meant she was only fifty-nine years old now.

She was only a little bit older than Chuck had been the night he'd looked for her in the waves.

But already, she was here in the retirement facility.

It wasn't fair.

Chuck returned to his suite and closed the door behind him. After a dramatic pause, during which he stood, heavy with thought, his hand still on the doorknob, he checked his phone to find numerous texts from loved ones. Oriana had, of course, sent him the most.

But Estelle had messaged him, too.

Estelle: Thank you for letting me crash for a little while. I hope you haven't been bothered by all my prying. I promise I'll leave you alone from here on out. You don't want to talk about your lighthouse keeper friend, and I don't really want to talk about my writing process, either. It's good that we can respect each other's privacy. Have a wonderful rest of your night.

Chuck's heart slammed in his chest. He didn't know what to think. On the one hand, he wanted to let sleeping dogs lie. On the other hand, Estelle was opening her heart to him. And maybe she had the research skills to get to the bottom of this.

He certainly couldn't do it himself.

Chapter Nine

1982

Chuck watched helplessly as the French teenager Vivian was carried on a stretcher to the awaiting ambulance. She'd just lost consciousness, and her mother was out of her mind with worry, alternating between howls of fear and stricken silences. She boarded the ambulance with Vivian. Chuck made eye contact with her as the doors were shut between them. It seemed clear that he would never see her again, that their strange story was over. The ambulance burst out of the harbor, following the others that had already left, taking other shipwreck survivors off to the hospital.

Chuck shivered and crossed his arms. The fear and adrenaline he'd felt out on the water, looking for Vivian and other survivors, crashed in on him. He thought he might throw up.

It was then Chuck realized Clarence, the lighthouse keeper, remained beside him, stroking his grizzled beard. Chuck wasn't sure if Clarence remembered him, either.

The night had taken its toll. Around them, members of the Coast Guard hustled, talking about what they'd do about the wreck once the sun came up. They ignored Chuck and Clarence. They weren't needed anymore.

Chuck had the sudden and colossal urge to run home and gather his daughters and wife around him. He wanted to hug them and make sure they were safe.

Chuck caught Clarence's eye. Clarence gave a firm nod as though he understood and pulled his keys out of his pocket. "Let's go," he said.

There was nothing left to see.

Clarence and Chuck got into Clarence's truck and drove through the inky-black night. The moon had fallen once more behind the clouds. Chuck wondered if Travis was doing all right in the lighthouse and prayed there wouldn't be another accident out on the water. Maybe Travis wasn't experienced enough to handle the lighthouse position. Maybe Clarence was naive to think he could leave him alone for even a few minutes.

"What kind of ship was that?" Chuck asked, his voice barely heard over the truck's engine.

"It looked like a cruise ship to me," Clarence said.

"A cruise ship? This late in October in New England?" Chuck shook his head. It wasn't impossible, but it was rather unlikely. Tourism season was over. And most people didn't appreciate a sail on the stormy seas unless there was a promise of warm sun the following morning.

Clarence grunted as though he didn't know and didn't care and turned onto Chuck's street. Chuck wanted to ask Clarence if he thought there were many casualties, but he wasn't sure how Clarence could possibly know that when Chuck didn't know himself.

Clarence pulled the truck into the driveway and kept the engine on. Chuck reached over to shake Clarence's hand. "It was a heck of a night," he said gravely.

He didn't say it was a pleasure to meet you because he wasn't sure he felt it.

"It was good of you to find the girl," Clarence said. "Come back and see us at the lighthouse sometime. It gets awfully lonely up there."

Chuck said he would although he couldn't imagine it right now.

Clarence backed the truck out of the driveway and disappeared around the corner, leaving Chuck in the darkness of his front yard, standing in the cold wind like a fool. Again, he had an out-of-body experience, remembering that this was his front yard rather than the one he'd built and cultivated in Nantucket. He couldn't go back there. This was home.

It felt like whiplash.

What time was it? Two? Three? It felt as though he'd time traveled.

Chuck got to the front door and turned the knob. It was locked, which was strange. They never locked it because they trusted all their neighbors, and it wasn't tourist season, so nobody strange was milling about. He certainly hadn't locked it himself. But when he'd left, he'd gone through the back, and he remembered now. So he headed around the side, through the fence, and tried the back door. But that was locked, too. He was suddenly stumped. He couldn't breathe. Standing on the back porch, he gazed up at his pitch-black house and considered what to do.

Of course, he could bang on the door and wake everyone up. He imagined Oriana and Meghan sobbing, asking him where he'd been and why he was acting so scary. He imagined Mia's eyes.

But that was when it occurred to him. Mia was the only one who could have locked the door. It meant that Mia had woken up, seen he was gone, and locked him out. Maybe she knew he hadn't taken his keys.

His palms were clammy. Tears sprang to his eyes.

Does she want me out already? I just moved to Martha's Vineyard to be with her! he wondered, his stomach heaving.

It hadn't occurred to him that he could be rejected like this. And why was that? Was he really so arrogant to believe he could have whatever he wanted?

Then again, hadn't he only begun his affair after he'd learned that Margaret had cheated on him first?

But what kind of life was that? he wondered. Was he perpetually on the hunt for revenge? He was a child.

But none of these anxious thoughts would get him inside where it was warm.

Chuck checked all the windows on the ground floor. They were locked tightly. There was no way in.

What could he do?

Despondent and out of his mind, Chuck walked back down the beach toward the lighthouse. Its comforting light went over his face and ducked back through the night before returning. The walk there felt familiar now, as though he'd done it far more than once.

Clarence's truck was parked out front. This time, Travis was outside, staring out at the water, smoking a cigarette. Chuck wanted to tell him to quit, saying that it was awful for him. But he guessed that Travis was smoking one of his father's cigarettes and that his father had given him the cigarette freely. Chuck couldn't go against Travis's father, not in matters of parenting.

"He's angry with me," Travis said as Chuck approached. He didn't seem surprised to see him again. "He thinks I wasn't paying attention properly. He says I should have seen the boat before it started really sinking."

Chuck wanted to say that Clarence was the real light-house keeper, not him. It was his responsibility. He shouldn't blame his child for not seeing the shipwreck right away!

Chuck hated that Clarence put the blame on Travis's shoulders. When Chuck was a teenager, his own father acted similarly, and Chuck felt the weight of a thousand tons.

Instead of saying all that, though, Chuck shook his head and offered, "It was a dramatic night. I'm sure your dad said a lot of things he doesn't really mean."

Travis puffed his cigarette and looked down at the sand. It was clear he'd failed some kind of test.

Chuck considered telling Travis that his wife had locked him out, but he didn't know why. But it wouldn't really be the truth. He knew why Mia was upset.

She didn't trust him.

Why would she ever trust him?

"I'm headed home," Travis said.

"I thought you lived here," Chuck said, gesturing to the lighthouse.

"My dad does," Travis said. "But we have a little house by the woods, too. That's where I stay most days. And I guess my old man won't let me handle the light-house by myself anymore. Not now." He kicked the sand and looked as though he wanted to say something else but didn't.

Again, Chuck considered asking Travis whether he went to high school or had plans to leave the island and go to college. But it seemed as plain as day that Travis didn't have plans beyond going to bed within the hour.

"Could you take me to the hospital?" Chuck said because he couldn't think of anywhere else to go, and he didn't feel like heading up into the lighthouse to find Clarence brooding and staring out at the black ocean.

"You want to check on them?" Travis asked, furrowing his brow.

Chuck's chest ached. He wanted to know if Vivian was all right. Head wounds were heinous; they could turn on you at a moment's notice and knock you unconscious again. He prayed his rescue mission hadn't been for nothing.

Travis and Chuck got into Clarence's truck. It was just forty minutes since Clarence had driven Chuck back home. Chuck was emotionally and physically exhausted. It was hard to remember why he couldn't sleep earlier in the night. Now, he felt as though he could sleep for days.

Travis pulled into the parking lot at the hospital and parked.

"You don't have to come in with me," Chuck said as he unbuckled his seat belt.

"I don't have anything better to do." Travis shrugged.

Travis and Chuck entered the hospital at four o'clock in the morning. A few people who looked to be the shipwreck survivors sat in the waiting room, sleeping on one another's shoulders. Chuck assessed them, remembering what Clarence had said about them being on a cruise ship. It was true that they looked wealthy or as wealthy as shipwreck victims could look. Their hair had dried strangely, and they looked gray-faced and upset.

Feeling a jolt of bravery, Chuck strode to the front counter. "Hi, I'm here to check on a relative of mine. Her name is Vivian. She came in with the rest of the ship-wreck survivors."

The woman at the front desk arched her eyebrow. "We haven't been able to put everyone in the system yet. There are so many of them and so few of us."

Chuck's heartbeat fluttered. "Of course."

"Why don't you wait for a while? I'll come find you when we know more," she said.

Chuck turned to Travis, ready to suggest that he head home. Maybe Chuck could get a cab when the sun came up. He would spend the time preparing his story for Mia until then. Nothing of the story was false; it was all terribly true. Although it sounded made up, all she had to do was call the hospital or the Coast Guard to get confirmation or read it in the newspaper.

Maybe that meant it was better for Chuck to go home after the news flowed across the island and got to Mia first.

"Oh! Monsieur!" a voice rang out through the waiting room.

Chuck twisted around to see Vivian's mother racing toward him with her arms extended. Her eyes were frantic. She threw her arms around him again and shook with sorrow.

"She will not wake up," she cried. "I cannot understand."

It took Chuck less than a minute to realize that the mother—whose name was Natasha, he learned—didn't speak enough English to understand what the doctors were saying about Vivian. He and Travis followed her through the glossy white halls of the hospital to the trauma ward, where Vivian was unconscious and in bed. Natasha shook with fear and frequently let out sobs of alarm.

Chuck was beginning to think it was fate that he hadn't been able to get back into his house. He'd been needed here.

But how would he translate everything back to Natasha? He spun around and looked at Travis. "Do you speak any French?" he asked.

Travis gaped at him. "Why would I know any French?"

It was an honest question, but even Chuck recognized how ignorant it had been. "Never mind," he said, taking Travis's shoulder.

Natasha tugged his hand and led him deeper into the hospital. Perhaps because he didn't know what else to do, Travis followed. They soon found themselves outside Vivian's room, behind a big window, looking down on the girl. She was peaceful, her eyes closed tenderly, and her head wrapped with bandages. It looked as though she could wake up at any time.

Natasha waved to a doctor and said a lot of stuff in French, followed by, "This man? He saved Vivian's life."

Chuck felt a blush crawl up his arms and chest. He spoke directly to the doctor. "It wasn't just me. We got lucky." He wet his lips. "She doesn't understand everything you're saying, I guess?"

The doctor shook his head gravely. "I'm not sure how to make her understand. But her daughter is in a coma, and we don't know when she's going to wake up."

Chuck gaped at him, recognizing the horror of what he had to do next. Somehow, he had to translate this devastating news to the poor woman beside him.

"Do you have anything else I can pass along to her?" Chuck asked. "Anything that resembles good news?"

"Vivian is stable," the doctor said, palming the back of his neck. "She's young and fit, which will help her down the line, especially if the coma goes on too long and she has to relearn how to use her arms and legs."

Chuck took a staggered breath. Beside him, Natasha grabbed his elbow and squeezed it hard.

In French, she said something that sounded to him like tell me what's going on! Now! Although he couldn't be sure.

How could Chuck pass on this news in a language he didn't speak or understand?

"Thank you, Doctor," Chuck said, backing up.

The doctor sped off to tend to other patients. His eyes glinted with fear. Chuck had to guess that it was one of the more frantic late-night shifts at the Martha's Vineyard hospital, a place that calmed down by nearly ninety percent when the tourists left for the season. There was nobody around—usually—to have accidents or get into drunken fights.

Now, Chuck led Natasha to the chairs alongside her daughter's bed. Natasha was shaking. It was as though she'd forgotten that she'd asked Chuck to translate for her. Maybe she'd gotten the hint.

Chuck considered how he could translate what she needed to know. She wrapped both hands around one of his and stared at her daughter. The color drained from her cheeks.

"Natasha?" Chuck said.

Natasha shifted her eyes dreamily toward his. Was she listening? He couldn't tell.

"Very sick," Chuck decided to say of Vivian. "She must sleep for a long time."

Tears welled in Natasha's eyes. She nodded furiously as though she understood. But how could she? Slowly, she returned her attention to Vivian and reached across to touch Vivian's hand, which was connected to several clear tubes.

Something caught Chuck's attention. He turned to find Travis Knight still in the window, gazing down at Vivian. He looked captivated, as though he'd traveled a great distance to be here and save the day. He looked like a young man in love.

But Travis and Vivian were from separate universes. Even more than that, Vivian was now in the land of sleep, and Travis was wide awake, watching over her. They would probably never meet.

Chapter Ten

Present Day

Roland had urged Estelle not to hurry back to Nantucket so late on a snowy evening. It meant she was "trapped" on Martha's Vineyard for the night, cozied up at her friend Margorie Tomlinson's place. Margorie was the romance novelist who'd accused Estelle of plagiarism last year, launching a multi-pronged attack on Estelle's career that catapulted both of them to international stardom. Perhaps the fact that they'd so recently been enemies should have kept Estelle away. But in the wake of that horror, she and Margorie had found common ground, frequently renting little cabins on the water in various places for "writing retreats," talking about characters and story ideas and giving one another advice.

Now, Estelle and Margorie were on the sofa with glasses of red wine and a big bowl of popcorn between them. Estelle was telling Margorie bits and pieces of her lighthouse keeper-themed romance, which Margorie was fascinated by.

"My father-in-law hinted that he has intel on a lighthouse keeper," Estelle finished, "but he won't tell me a thing about him! Imagine being ninety-three and gate-keeping all your stories!"

Margorie's eyes were stormy. "Why would he do that?"

"It's puzzling," Estelle agreed, taking a handful of popcorn. "My only theory is that there's bad blood between him and this lighthouse keeper. He doesn't want the story to get out?"

"No offense to Chuck, but that's silly," Margorie offered. "Both islands know plenty of horrible things about Chuck Coleman. We know plenty of horrible things about everyone else, too. He's not alone in that. I mean, come on! Just look at what I did to you last year! Everyone knows about that, too."

"Oh, stop it. You know I don't care about that anymore. But Chuck's guilt is pretty powerful, I think," Estelle agreed, thinking of Chuck's affair and the ways it dramatically altered the generations to come. "But you're right. How could whatever happened with the lighthouse keeper be any worse than that?"

"Have you looked into this Clarence lighthouse keeper person?" Margorie asked. "The one Henry talked about?"

"I googled him in your driveway," Estelle admitted with a laugh. "There isn't much information. I was thinking I could go to the Martha's Vineyard Historical Society tomorrow before I get on the ferry."

"Good idea." Margorie snapped her fingers.

From upstairs came the sound of Margorie's fiancé Daniel's speaker. He was listening to the Beatles. Margorie laughed and said, "Daniel is obsessed with his new athletic regime. He does one hundred push-ups, one hundred sit-ups, and one hundred jumping jacks every day without fail."

Estelle whistled. "I'm impressed. When did he start?"

"The day after Thanksgiving." Margorie laughed. "Four days ago."

"That's four days longer than I'd keep that up," Estelle said. "How's the bookstore?"

Daniel owned and operated a bookstore on Martha's Vineyard and was, incidentally, best friends with Meghan, Roland's little half sister. Estelle knew that Margorie, Daniel, Meghan, and Meghan's husband, Hugo, frequently hung out together, grabbing dinner and going to films. Sometimes Margorie and Daniel were invited to Coleman family parties. They'd been more than welcome on Thanksgiving, but Margorie and Daniel had other plans.

"The bookstore is in the black!" Margorie said, her hands raised in praise. "It was a difficult spring, but as soon as the tourists started swarming in, the books flew off the shelves. Oh! Daniel wants to do another book signing with the two of us if you're up for that. He was thinking late spring when everyone comes back. Our feud always gives the bookstore a boost."

"I love selling and signing books!" Estelle said with a laugh. "You know I'd take any excuse to do it with you by my side."

"You flatter me!" Margorie said with a laugh.

Just then, Estelle's phone buzzed and buzzed. She hunted through the blanket on the sofa to find it and was surprised to see Chuck's name. "One second," she said, snapping up from the sofa to answer it. "Hello?"

Chuck's breathing was ragged. For a moment, Estelle was really frightened that something was wrong.

"Estelle, hi," Chuck said finally.

"Are you all right, Chuck?" Estelle tried to keep her voice bright and chipper.

"I'm just fine," Chuck said. But to Estelle, he sounded as though he'd just seen a ghost. "I wanted to apologize for my behavior earlier today. I feel I wasn't entirely kind or open with you."

Estelle furrowed her brow and gave Margorie a look. Margorie raised her eyebrows with curiosity. She mouthed, "What is he saying?"

"It's really okay," Estelle said to Chuck. "Like I said in my text, I'll stop bothering you about the lighthouse keeper. The past is in the past. I can do my own research. It's better this way, anyway."

Chuck cleared his throat. Estelle half expected him to hang up the phone.

But then he said, "There's been a strange development in the story."

Estelle furrowed her brow. "What do you mean?"

"I don't want to explain over the phone," Chuck said.

Estelle stuttered. "I'm still on the Vineyard. I can swing by tomorrow morning if you like?"

"Okay." Chuck sounded cagey. "I appreciate that, Estelle. Really." He paused. "I hope you don't think I'm being a crazy old man."

"I would never think that," Estelle promised to head over by eight the following morning. Chuck hung up the phone without saying goodbye.

Estelle gaped at Margorie as her heart pounded.

"What was that about?" Margorie demanded.

"He wants to talk." Estelle shrugged. "I guess I'll let him talk?"

Margorie grinned. "It's all you can do."

* * *

Estelle got up the following morning to have coffee with Margorie and Daniel before they each headed off in their separate directions: Daniel to the bookstore, Margorie to her writing office down the hall, and Estelle to Chuck's retirement facility to learn about this "strange development" in Chuck's story. Estelle felt shivery with anticipation. She drank one too many cups of coffee and ate half a blueberry muffin, asking Daniel questions about his bookstore to distract herself.

Estelle parked in the lot in front of the retirement facility and pulled out her phone to see a missed call from Hilary, plus a message that read: I'm just panicking about wedding stuff. I'll call Sam and blab to her instead! Love you.

Estelle smiled to herself, thinking of the beautiful celebrations in the very near future. She texted back, promising to call later, then raised her chin as she strode into the retirement facility and headed back to Chuck's suite. En route, she passed the younger woman in the wheelchair, who seemed to stare straight ahead no matter what. It seemed unlikely she could communicate at all.

Chuck opened the door before Estelle had a chance to knock. It felt as though he'd been waiting for her, listening for her footsteps. Estelle was taken aback. He was paler, even more so than yesterday, and it looked as though he'd tugged at his collared shirt so much that it hung off his neck.

"Chuck?" Estelle breathed. "Are you all right?"

Chuck paced back and forth in front of his chair. Estelle wished Roland was here to calm him down. But maybe Chuck didn't want whatever this was getting back to Roland. Perhaps it was another secret.

"I can't say," Chuck offered finally. "But it's such a funny coincidence, Estelle. It really is." He stopped short and looked at her. His eyes were bloodshot. "What are the chances she'd appear the same weekend you brought up lighthouses? Something so innocuous as lighthouses?"

Estelle gaped at him. "Who appeared, Chuck?"

Chuck sat down, hung his head, and touched his ears. Estelle considered if she should call a nurse.

"You mentioned the accident in 1982," Chuck breathed. "The shipwreck."

Estelle sat down across from him and cupped her knees. She didn't say anything.

"Clarence Knight was the lighthouse keeper at the time," Chuck continued. "But he wasn't the only person in the lighthouse when the ship was sinking. His teenage son, Travis, was there, too. As was I."

Estelle's eyes widened.

"When we realized what was happening, Clarence called the Coast Guard, and Clarence and I sped off for the docks to see how we could help. There was a French woman there. She was incredibly upset, obviously, but she was crying so much more than all the others. It took a second to realize what was wrong with her. She told me her daughter was still out there. We sped out into the dark water. I was calling Vivian's name as loudly as I could. It's nothing short of a miracle that we found her. But soon after we got back to shore, we realized she'd hit her head hard at some point on the water. She fell into a coma."

Estelle pressed her hand over her mouth. Chuck's shoulders began to shake.

"I've thought about that night often over the years," Chuck said. "That night had incredible ramifications for the rest of my life. It's difficult to explain." He pressed his lips into a line, and Estelle understood that he wouldn't be sharing what those ramifications had been. Maybe it was better not to know. "But the other night, a woman was checked into the retirement facility. A woman in a wheel-chair. A woman far too young for a place like this." Chuck's eyes glinted. "I didn't want to believe it at first. But now I'm almost one hundred percent clear on the matter. The woman in the wheelchair and the teenage girl we pulled out of the water in 1982 are one and the same. She now has the same last name as the lighthouse keeper and his son. But I don't know why."

He raised his head and gazed at Estelle. Estelle had the sensation that she was peering through his eyes and into the past.

"There's so much about the modern world I don't understand," Chuck said. "But I know there are ways to research what happened, where Travis and his father ended up, and why Vivian is here at the retirement home by herself."

Estelle's mind opened like a window. He wanted her help.

Chuck extended his hand. "Maybe this is too distracting for you. It might take you too far away from your novel."

But Estelle shook her head. "It's too fascinating to walk away from."

The corners of Chuck's lips curved upward. "There's so much I never understood about this story because of what happened in my own," he said.

Again, Estelle burned with the desire to understand what he meant. What had happened? Back in 1982, Chuck married his second wife and raised ten-year-old Oriana and seven-year-old Meghan. He'd probably been reeling with regret for past mistakes. Whatever drama lurked within Vivian and the shipwreck story probably proved too much for him.

Maybe he'd had to turn his back and tend to his own messes.

Estelle didn't wait around. She understood that Chuck wanted her to get to the bottom of what happened to Vivian as soon as she could. She promised she'd call Chuck when she knew more and struck back out of his suite, passing by Vivian Knight in her wheelchair. According to Chuck, Vivian had been born in France and, for whatever reason, had been on a ship that had sunk off the coast of Martha's Vineyard forty-three years ago. She'd been seventeen.

Now, she sat quietly, watching another rom-com as nurses and other folks who lived in the retirement facility milled around her.

It felt like a tragedy.

Chapter Eleven

E stelle called Roland from her car to check on things at home. He answered, breathing raggedly, and said, "Just got back from a five-mile run!"

Estelle smiled into the phone, imagining him glistening with sweat in the kitchen, drinking a big glass of water. "Isn't it freezing outside?"

"Not once you really get going," Roland said. "Are you on your way back?"

"Not quite," Estelle admitted. "I ran into a few potential story ideas and got sidetracked."

"It sounds like it's going well, then?" Estelle could hear Roland's smile through the receiver. "I know how you get when you're obsessed with a story. Will I see you before Christmas?"

Estelle laughed. "I'll be home tonight, I think," she said.

"Where's the next stop?" Roland asked.

"The Martha's Vineyard Historical Society," she explained.

"Uh-oh. You're getting your hands dirty," he said.

"I'm already up to my ears in crazy stories!" Estelle offered.

"Can't wait to hear them," Roland said. "I love you. Drive safe, okay?"

Estelle promised she would.

Estelle drove to downtown Oaks Bluff and parked outside the Martha's Vineyard Historical Society. She'd been to the Nantucket Historical Society what felt like hundreds of times, and the Martha's Vineyard Historical Society was almost an exact replica, save for the fact that its documents, old newspapers, and photographs were of different sets of people from a different timeline of events. A woman behind the counter introduced herself as Amy and showed Estelle around, telling her she could use the computer to look up anything in their database. Nobody else was in there, which clearly upset Amy. She said, "Those ancestral websites made it easy for people to research their families online. It's tragic, really. It's made everyone obsessed with their own stories rather than the island's history and how all those stories come together." She sat back down behind the desk and looked at her hands as though she was frightened she'd said too much.

Estelle thanked her. "I'll probably be here all morning long!"

This seemed to brighten Amy's mood. "Let me know what you need! I'm happy to help."

Estelle decided her first big clue was the shipwreck. Feeling like a woman in a spy novel, she searched newspaper archives for a while until she discovered the first article published about the shipwreck. The headline read: BILLIONAIRE CRUISE SHIP SINKS OFF COAST OF MARTHA'S VINEYARD.

Billionaire? Estelle's ears rang. She kept reading.

Billionaire Roger Albright is reported as "missing" after a shipwreck off the coast of Martha's Vineyard took the lives of twelve passengers. Lighthouse keeper Clarence Knight made the call at eleven forty-five, reporting that a large cruise ship was bow-under. The Coast Guard sprang into action immediately and was able to save thirty-nine other passengers as well as one dog. It is still unclear why and how the ship sank, although some blame the storms that raged through the Atlantic that night. The investigation is ongoing.

It seems likely that billionaire Roger Albright's four children will receive their inheritance of three hundred million each.

The youngest passenger aboard the vessel, French teenager Vivian Morceau, remains in a coma in the wake of the accident. Doctors at Martha's Vineyard hospital maintain their belief she will wake up "any day now."

Estelle leaned back in her chair and crossed her arms over her chest. Through the window, she could see the Oak Bluffs historical carousel, spinning round and round. A winter sun blared in a cerulean sky.

But she couldn't pull herself away from the tremendous mysteries before her.

She'd heard the name Roger Albright before although she couldn't remember why. Perhaps the fact that he'd died so famously and tragically off the coast of Martha's Vineyard had implanted his name in islanders' minds forever.

Estelle continued to read. She wanted to answer the article's question: Why did the ship sink? The investigation, as they said, was ongoing.

Estelle found numerous articles that discussed the shipwreck. Their headlines read:

BILLIONAIRE DEEMED DEAD AFTER SHIPWRECK

DOOMED CRUISE TAKES ANOTHER LIFE

WHERE WAS THE CRUISE GOING? EXPERTS DISAGREE

WHAT CAUSED THE WRECK? PASSENGERS ARE CAGEY

Estelle's curiosity was piqued. Based on her reading, it seemed that the passengers of the cruise ship—which was called *La Boheme*—were unable or unwilling to say what the destination of the cruise ship was, nor how they thought the ship had gone under. Several journalists suggested that the passengers were simply "too upset" or "traumatized" after the wreck, but Estelle didn't think that seemed likely. How easy was it to just say where the boat had been going? It didn't make sense.

Estelle soon felt she was hitting a brick wall. Bit by bit, journalists from 1982, 1983, and even 1984 gave up on figuring out what had happened with the shipwreck. Very soon after, all four of Roger Albright's children received their inheritance and probably went off to live their wealthy lives and do whatever they pleased. It was as though the story, the shipwreck, and Roger Albright's death were abandoned. Once the eighties ended, all interest in the shipwreck ceased to exist.

Estelle was mystified.

It was now midafternoon. Amy came with a cup of coffee and a bag of pretzels, which Estelle thanked her for.

"You haven't left to eat anything!" Amy said. "I was worried about your blood sugar."

Estelle laughed and raked her fingers through her hair. The edge of her vision was blurry. But she wanted to hold on just a little bit longer. All she'd found thus far were more questions. She needed at least one answer before she sped back to Nantucket.

Finally, she searched for marriage records during the eighties. The database didn't bring up very many Vivians —just five over the course of fifty years. One of them was Vivian Morceau, who'd married Travis Knight in 1984— two years after the accident. There was even a photograph attached to the file. The kids in the photo couldn't have been older than nineteen or twenty. They glowed with optimism and health that seemed completely foreign to the woman who sat in a wheelchair by herself at the retirement facility. Estelle's heart swelled. She took a picture of the photograph for safekeeping and put everything away.

Before she left, Estelle checked on Clarence and Travis Knight. She was curious who Travis's mother was; she wondered what had happened to them. It looked like Clarence had passed away in Providence twelve years ago. But there was no record of Travis's death. Beyond that, Travis had been born in the mid-sixties to Clarence and a young woman named Sarah. There wasn't much information on Sarah, save for the fact that she'd died two years after Travis's birth. Estelle took a breath and put the files away.

She had the sensation that she'd seen and learned too much in one day. She'd pored through too many documents—all of which indicated very real events in very real humans' lives.

She was grateful she'd never become a real researcher

or journalist. Wading through so many people's stories at once felt tremendously heavy. She wasn't sure how to carry them all in her head.

Chapter Twelve

1982

Impossibly, the sun came up the morning after the shipwreck and bathed the hospital halls in light. Chuck sat in the waiting area with his head in his hands. It sounded as though there was a gong between his ears, ringing every few seconds. He needed to get home. He needed to go to bed. But he was also terrified of what awaited him there. Mia had locked him out. She was angry. And if she decided she no longer wanted to be with him, what would he do? He couldn't go back to Nantucket Island. He wasn't wanted there, either.

Would he miss Oriana and Meghan growing up?

He muttered to himself, "Why am I such a bad person?" He felt rattled and embarrassed; he felt flummoxed by life's many bashed hopes and dreams.

Suddenly, Travis reappeared in the waiting room. Seeing him again was almost a surprise since he'd left the waiting room several hours ago and disappeared somewhere in the hospital.

"You ready to go?" Travis asked, stretching his arms over his head.

Chuck followed Travis to the truck in the lot and buckled himself into the passenger seat. Travis didn't bother with a seat belt.

"The doctors still don't know if she'll be all right," Travis muttered, his eyes glazed. "I can't wrap my mind around that, you know? They're medical professionals. She clearly bumped her head just a little bit. There's hardly a mark. Why can't they pull themselves together? Why can't they give us answers?"

Chuck remembered the blood he had seen on Vivian's head at the docks but remained quiet. Travis needed to believe she was going to get well soon.

"Thanks for driving me up there," Chuck said as they neared his house.

"I appreciate you dragging me in there," Travis said. His eyes shone.

Chuck wanted to warn him of something. But he wasn't sure exactly why. Was he worried about Clarence? About Vivian? About Travis's lack of direction in life?

But nothing about the past twelve hours was normal. That was clear.

"Take care," Chuck said. He got out of the truck and walked up to the front porch.

According to Chuck's watch, it was eight thirty in the morning, which meant that Oriana and Meghan were both in school and Mia was home, probably, or else at the store or tending to other errands. Like earlier, he tried the front door to find it locked. When he walked around the house, he discovered a full view of Mia in the kitchen window, sipping coffee and watching the water. At first, she didn't see him. He filled his lungs with air and considered just how beautiful she was. He felt more in love with her right now than he ever had been, and he thanked his lucky stars that he'd ever met her, that they'd had daughters together, and that he'd changed his entire life for her.

But then, her eyes snapped over to him, and her face transformed into a scowl.

Chuck's heart dropped into his stomach.

Mia stormed to the back door and began yelling at him through the glass. Chuck couldn't make out everything she said, but he caught a few words like "liar," "betrayal," and "I don't know why."

Chuck kept his mouth shut until Mia had run herself ragged. Her face was red with rage.

Chuck raised his hands and said, "Can I come inside so we can talk?" He wanted to be reasonable. He wanted to explain.

Mia huffed angrily and pulled the door open as though she guessed she couldn't keep him out of his house forever. She stomped back to the sink and continued to scrub a skillet, probably one she'd used to make eggs for the girls. She was such a good mother. She was always so on top of everything. Chuck was always lacking in the family department. Proof of that was the success of his business. It was like he could only have one or the other.

Chuck closed the door behind him and hovered in the living room, watching her through the kitchen doorway. He crossed his arms. "Mia, I can explain," he said softly.

Mia cut the water and dried her hands. She refused to look at him. "Do you know how terrified I was when I figured out you weren't in the house?"

Chuck took a deep breath. "I couldn't sleep."

"So you left the house? And then what? What did

you do, Chuck?" She sounded so accusatory and exhausted.

Chuck's heart slammed over and over. He wanted to tell her that he wouldn't cheat on her, that he would never cheat on her. But he knew she wouldn't believe him. He'd already cheated on Margaret with Mia. He'd already left Margaret for Mia. Who was to say he wouldn't do the same thing again and leave Mia behind?

Plus, it had been extraordinarily difficult for Mia to be the other woman for so long. Yes, she'd agreed to it initially, but that didn't mean it hadn't run her ragged. She'd been a part-time single mother, with Chuck only picking up the slack when he was able to. But that also meant she had far more ownership over the girls, what they did and how they thought. It meant the girls were far more comfortable when their mother was around than just their father.

"I went for a walk," Chuck said, fumbling over his words. "I went up to the lighthouse and met the lighthouse keeper. And..."

"You met the lighthouse keeper?" Mia looked aghast.

Chuck raised his eyebrows. Did she know the lighthouse keeper? Probably, he guessed. Everyone on this island knew each other. Clarence had probably been raised here, the same as Mia.

"I did," he said. "But not long after I got there, Clarence and I saw a ship sinking, and we had to call it in. It was frantic. We ended up going out on the harbor to help—"

Mia waved her hand. "What are you talking about?" She gaped at him in disbelief.

Chuck touched the top of his head. He felt woozy as if he might collapse at any minute. And then, there was a sound at the front door. He hurried through the house to find a newspaper on the front stoop. It was right on time.

Chuck spread the newspaper across the counter and gestured at the headline: CRUISE LINER *LA BOHEME* SINKS OFF COAST OF MARTHA'S VINEYARD. Mia's face transformed again.

While he had her attention, Chuck told her the story about Vivian, about how she'd almost drowned. Mia pressed her lips into a line and read more of the article, then returned her attention to the dishes. The tension in the kitchen faded.

"I can't believe it," Mia breathed because she'd read already that the owner of the cruise ship was missing and that, as of that morning, ten drowned victims had been pulled out of the water. It was one of the greatest tragedies in or around Martha's Vineyard in the twentieth century. "I'm so glad you went out to look for that teenager. Who knows what would have happened?" She placed her hands on her cheeks. Chuck knew that she was thinking of their daughters. Maybe she would never let them get on another boat again.

"It made me think about how grateful I am for my life here with you," Chuck added finally.

But Mia shot him a look that meant *don't push your luck. Don't lay it on too thick.*

"I just wish you wouldn't sneak around at night," she said finally, her voice like a string. "You chose us, remember? You moved in with us. Stay with us." She cut the water in the sink and gazed at him. "Please."

Chuck went upstairs and stood outside the doorways of Oriana's and Meghan's bedrooms. Their beds were made because Mia expected it every morning, but Meghan's room was chaotic with clothes and toys.

Oriana's was clean and organized, proof of the well-trimmed nature of her mind. Mia often spoke of Oriana's future as though it glowed with light and promise. But neither Mia nor Chuck nor the president himself could possibly say what tomorrow would bring.

Chuck had half a mind to drive to Oriana and Meghan's elementary school and take them out for the day. He wanted to make them grilled cheese sandwiches and watch their favorite movies. He wanted to teach them about all the fish in the ocean and birds in the sky. But Mia would never allow him to take them out of school for "no reason." *I just want them to know how much I love them. I want them to know I'll never abandon them.*

Mia might say, *You abandoned them weekly when they were growing up. You were always going back to Nantucket, where your "real life" was.*

When Chuck had decided to come to Martha's Vineyard for good, he'd thought Mia would forgive him and move on. He'd thought they'd build a beautiful life of forgiveness and joy.

He thought they'd leave the past behind.

But people were far more complicated than that. Mia was far more complex than that. It was part of the reason he'd fallen in love with her.

Chuck showered and considered what to do next with his day. Ordinarily, he'd already be at the office he'd recently rented in downtown Oak Bluffs. His employees were surely already in, performing the tasks he'd delegated. Maybe they were gossiping about the shipwreck over coffee and between spreadsheets, with no knowledge that their boss had been an integral part of the tragedy.

Chuck couldn't imagine going there this morning and

pretending he hadn't just experienced one of the strangest nights of his life.

Downstairs, Mia was mopping the kitchen and listening to the radio. The radio announcer spoke about the shipwreck and that the owner of the cruise liner was the very wealthy Roger Albright, whose four children were poised to inherit hundreds of millions of dollars. Chuck whistled, but Mia didn't look up from her task.

"Are you going to the office?" she asked.

"Yes," Chuck lied.

"Can you get home by seven?" Mia sniffed.

Chuck tilted his head with surprise. It was rare that Mia asked anything like this of him. Was she creating "parameters" for their marriage? Was she trying to box him in?

If so, how did he feel about that?

Chuck backed out of the driveway and into a startlingly sunny day. It was hard to remember the severity of last night's storm. Perhaps pretending his own lie to himself, Chuck drove downtown first, did a lap around the carousel near the harbor, then drove the rest of the way to the hospital. It had only been three hours since he'd been there, but it felt like another lifetime. Most of the cruise ship survivors had vacated the waiting room.

The same receptionist worked the front desk. Chuck strode up to her with a smile, and she smiled back, remembering him from earlier.

"How has it been?" he asked. "Did everyone get a place to stay?"

"The island has pulled out all the stops," she explained in a soft voice. "They've opened their hotels and bed-and-breakfasts and put everyone up for a few nights. It's sensational, isn't it? I just love this community."

Chuck breathed a sigh of relief, then remembered something, a question that had been on his mind since he'd read the article in the paper. "Did any of them tell you where they were headed?"

The receptionist shook her head. "The only information I got was 'south.' I think that billionaire wanted to flee northern winters."

"But it must have had a final destination in mind," Chuck said.

The receptionist raised her shoulders and answered the ringing phone.

Chuck went back upstairs to check on Natasha and Vivian. It wasn't lost on him that "Natasha" wasn't an incredibly French name, and he wondered if she had roots in Eastern Europe or Russia. Maybe, through her limited English, he could get a better sense of where the boat had been headed and why. *Not that it mattered*, he reminded himself. A tragedy happened. Specifics about the story weren't essential. Probably, nobody would make it down south for the winter, least of all the billionaire who'd been reported as "missing."

Chuck bowed his head. He had a hunch that Travis thought this meant "foul play." But what it really meant, he didn't say, was that Roger Albright had died, and they hadn't been able to confirm it. A shiver went down his spine.

"The strangest thing is," Travis said, "that when Natasha found out that Roger was missing, she went crazy. She was sobbing and throwing things. She looked genuinely frightened and angry."

Alarm bells rang in Chuck's mind. Maybe they'd been friends? Relatives?

Maybe they'd been lovers?

"Did you happen to hear where they were headed?" Chuck asked quietly.

"I heard somebody mention Puerto Rico," Travis said. His eyes glinted conspiratorially.

Chuck crossed and uncrossed his arms. He wondered how he could get to the bottom of what had happened. But then again, why did it matter? Natasha and Vivian were safe. The boat had sunk. Chuck had a young family to take care of. He had a business to run. Why was he suddenly obsessed with this case?

Mia was right.

"I'd better head out," Chuck said, feeling foolish. "I hope you'll keep me in the loop about Vivian and Natasha."

"Will do," Travis promised.

It was clear that Travis wasn't going anywhere for a while. He wanted to make sure Vivian was all right.

Chuck went back to the office and pretended to work until four that afternoon. During his walks through the desks of his employees, he overheard several of them talking about Roger Albright. This was how Chuck learned that Roger had made his money the same way Chuck did. He was marginally more successful than Chuck, but that meant nothing if he was dead.

Chuck suddenly felt a kinship with Roger.

He called his secretary into his office a few minutes before he left for the day. As he pulled his coat over his shoulders, he said, "Could you hire someone to gather information about Roger Albright and his business accounts?"

"Of course," his secretary said, giving him a strange look that Chuck decided not to reprimand her on. "I'll make a call now."

Chuck thanked her and strode back into the fading October afternoon. It suddenly occurred to him that Mia expected him at home, that she'd asked him to be there by seven. He pictured himself, Mia, Oriana, and Meghan cozied up in front of the television, enjoying one another's company. Perhaps Mia had already fully forgiven him for leaving the house last night. Perhaps they'd stay up later than usual, share a glass of wine, and talk in the way they once had—when they were first falling in love.

But when Chuck got home, he discovered that Mia's plans were far different.

Mia was already dressed up when he got there. She wore a sleek black dress and a pair of earrings, and she was careful not to mess up her makeup as she tended to Oriana and Meghan and helped them with their homework. Chuck approached to kiss Mia on the cheek, but she pulled away at the last second.

"I'm heading out," she explained to him. "Thanks for getting home early." Her tone was formal and strange.

Chuck gaped at her as she prepared to leave. She threw on her coat and flipped her hair out, grabbed her purse and kissed their daughters goodbye.

"Where are you going?" Chuck demanded.

"I have plans," she said. "I told you that."

"Bye, Mom!" Oriana and Meghan called, still focused on their homework.

Chuck didn't want to make a big scene in front of their daughters. He stood alone in the center of the kitchen, feeling like a fool.

The door slammed. Mia's engine started. Chuck sat at

the kitchen table and watched his daughters, their mouths moving as they wrote equations and spelling words.

He thought of Natasha at Vivian's bedside.

He thought about a world he would never be able to understand.

And he wondered, *Is Mia going to leave me? Has it already begun?*

Chapter Thirteen

Present Day

It was a few days after Estelle returned from Martha's Vineyard. There in her office, snow swirling out the window directly in front of her desk, Estelle typed notes to herself about the mystery of Clarence, the sunken ship, Travis, Roger Albright, and Vivian. Originally, she'd begun this "investigation" to flesh out her novel and inspire herself. But now, she felt captivated with unsolved mysteries—and why Vivian Morceau Knight currently sat alone and wordless at the retirement facility on Martha's Vineyard. Where was Travis? Why had the boat sank in the first place? Why had everyone abandoned the story as though it didn't matter at all?

But Estelle couldn't spend the rest of the day at her computer. It was December, and Christmas was just around the corner. Like every other year, she'd invited her daughters, sister-in-law, daughter-in-law, and female granddaughters over to bake cookies, drink wine, and chat. It was one of her most anticipated events of the year —a time when she fully embraced being a "grandmother." Ida and her daughters Frankie and Nellie were coming this year, too. It would be a full house. Estelle had bought plenty of baking supplies and bottles of red wine.

Estelle went downstairs to find Roland at the kitchen island with a bottle of beer and a newspaper spread out in front of him. She kissed him on the cheek, barely distracting him from his crossword, and said, "You remember the girls are coming over?"

"I'm more than ready to let them take over the house!" Roland raised his beer. "I just have three more words left..."

Estelle peered over his shoulder, but Roland smacked his hand over the crossword before she could see anything. "You're a writer, Estelle," he said playfully. "This kind of thing is easy for you. Give the old man a chance, okay?"

Estelle giggled. It was true that Roland usually got angry when she tried to help him with his crossword. She began to get things out of the cupboards, such as flour and sugar, oats, and chocolate chips. As soon as Roland went upstairs, she put on Christmas music and prepared her heart. A few seconds later, the doorbell rang. But Sam didn't wait for Estelle to come open it before she strode in, bellowing, "Hello! We're here!"

Estelle hurried out to hug Sam and Darcy. Rachelle had gone back to Italy until next year, which devastated all of them. It would be the first Christmas she'd miss. Estelle just prayed that she'd get all that travel out of her system and not miss any more.

Darcy waddled into the kitchen and sat down in front of the cookie cutters, her hand over her pregnant belly.

Sam took a tortilla chip from a bowl Estelle had put out and assessed the bags and bags of ingredients. "It looks like we have our work cut out for us!"

Estelle laughed.

"Hilary called me this morning," Sam said, snapping her hands over her thighs. "She's having a little bit of a panic about the wedding."

Estelle was surprised at herself. She hadn't thought about Hilary's wedding in ages! She'd been too immersed in the story of the sunken ship.

"We'll help her with whatever she needs," Estelle promised, feeling like the worst mother ever.

"You know how she is," Sam said. "She likes to worry too much. It's her way of making sure everything falls into place."

The doorbell rang again. This time, Hilary and Aria ambled in with piles of wedding magazines and stressed-out smiles. Estelle hugged Hilary extra tight and ordered her to sit down. But as soon as Hilary collapsed in the chair beside Darcy, she burst into all kinds of drama about the wedding. "The caterer pulled out," she said, "and it's going to take so much time to find a new one up to par with the old one! I wish Rachelle could come back and do it." She sighed and looked down at her fingernails, which she'd tugged at and bit. Estelle couldn't remember Aria ruining her nails since she was a child. It meant things were especially bad.

Estelle made everyone cups of tea and tried to impart as much wisdom as she could. "I'll be with you every step of the way," she told Hilary. "If it comes to it, I'll cater the thing myself."

"No way, Mom! I want you to have a good time." Hilary's shoulders fell.

As Hilary continued rambling about the wedding and all its drama, more and more Colemans came by— Shawna and Sheila and Marcy, plus Katrina and Ida and Nellie and Frankie. After a stressful year of ups and downs, of fears and tribulations, Ida and Frankie looked especially bright-eyed and optimistic. Estelle hugged them tightly and ordered them to put on aprons as she was nearly done mixing the cookie dough, which meant it was almost time to cut out the Christmas cookies. From the speaker, Nat King Cole sang with his full heart and soul.

After everything settled down, Sam turned everything on its head and asked Estelle how she'd been. Estelle, being the grandmother there to take care of everyone else, hadn't anticipated the conversation shifting to her. She stopped rolling out the dough and blinked. The only thing on her mind was the shipwreck, obviously.

"I've been doing research about old lighthouse keepers in Nantucket and Martha's Vineyard," she explained. "And it's led me into quite an intriguing true story."

She told them everything she'd learned thus far about the shipwreck, which wasn't a whole lot. "It feels like the twenty-first century all but abandoned the story," she said. "I can't get very far."

Suddenly, all the color drained from Darcy's face so much that Estelle was frightened that something was wrong with the baby.

"Darcy! Are you all right?" She turned from her dough and prepared to reach for her phone.

But Darcy's answer was a smile. "Wait. Are you

talking about the *La Boheme*? The cruise ship that sank in 1982?"

Estelle's heart hammered. "Yes?"

"I listened to a podcast about it!" Darcy explained.

"A podcast?" This was a medium Estelle hadn't ever fully explored. Her world was books and the occasional film. Why would you want to listen to someone talking at you?

Darcy nodded eagerly. "It was a mystery podcast. It outlined everything we know about the case, plus the twists and turns that happened afterward."

"Twists and turns?" Estelle repeated. She felt out of her mind. How could she have missed the twists and turns!?

"Nobody ever found out why the ship sank," Darcy said. "But some stuff may or may not have happened after the 'accident.'" She used air quotes to say *accident*. "Some of the stories are rumors, but it's almost impossible to say what's real and what isn't.

"Like, maybe you read that Roger Albright had an enormous inheritance," Darcy said excitedly.

"Yes! It went to his four children," Estelle finished.

"But there's a rumor that he had a fifth child," Darcy said. "It's also rumored that Roger Albright wanted to give everything to this fifth child and write his four legitimate children out of the will."

"That's a motive if I've ever heard one," Estelle said, raising her eyebrows.

"Right?" Darcy sighed. "But after Roger died, the money went to his four legitimate children, and nobody ever came forward to demand the fifth inheritance."

"So nobody knows who the fifth child was?" Sam asked.

Darcy shook her head. "Nobody ever knew! At least, it sounded like the story was totally abandoned after a while. Somehow, the investigation was botched."

"Was it Martha's Vineyard police who botched it?" Sam asked.

"That's not clear," Darcy said. It seemed nothing was.

"How do you sink a ship on purpose?" Estelle demanded. "Isn't it way too dangerous to experiment with something like that?"

"The total inheritance was in the billions of dollars," Darcy remembered. "I guess there's a price for everything. That's enough for someone out there."

Estelle returned her attention to the cookie dough as her family members continued gossiping about the shipwreck, Roger Albright and his four children, and his fifth illegitimate one. Eventually, Sam pulled up an article about where the Albright children were now. This brought Estelle away from the cookie dough, swapping places with Marcy and Sheila, who took over.

Sam showed Estelle a website with four photographs of the Albright children. They were now in their seventies and held prominent positions on art museum boards and at the heads of major broadcast companies. One of them had become a philanthropist, which Estelle knew was just a fancy way of saying you had more money than you knew what to do with.

It was hard to believe these people had ever been involved in some kind of sinister plot.

"Is it really possible that they had their father killed?" Estelle breathed.

"Rich people love money," Darcy said.

"Is this all for your book?" Hilary asked, pouring a

glass of wine for herself and smiling. "It sounds like it's turning into a murder mystery."

"Maybe you've changed genres!" Sam agreed. "Goodbye to romance, hello to drama!"

"I'd never turn my back on romance," Estelle said. "I'm still going to write the romance about the lighthouse keeper. Maybe there's a mystery element, but love is still at the core of the story. I can't escape that."

"What will your readers think of all that mystery and darkness?" Sam asked.

"I never know what they'll think," Estelle said quietly, thinking of her thousands of readers at home, some of whom had written her in hopeful expectation, asking when her next book would be finished.

But Estelle still hadn't told her daughters and grand-daughters the most mysterious facet of the story—a young woman who'd been aboard that ship the night it sank was now sitting wordlessly at Chuck's retirement facility. Chuck needed to know what had happened to her, why she was there, and where her family was. He'd asked Estelle for help.

Why was Chuck so curious about her? He'd said he'd been there the night *La Boheme* had sank and never figured out what happened with Vivian and Travis. He'd said that night had ramifications for his own life. But what did that mean?

Estelle didn't want to turn the Coleman women against Chuck. He'd just re-entered their lives. She'd keep her lips sealed.

"Let's put the first sheet of cookies in the oven!" Estelle suggested.

Estelle watched as Marcy bent to position the cookie sheet in the hot oven. Soon, Hilary asked Shawna for her opinion on a table-setting piece for the wedding, and the Coleman women were otherwise distracted.

This left Estelle to stew in the story, lost in her own mind. What made Estelle think she could get to the bottom of it if Darcy and the podcasters couldn't? She was no researcher. She was just a storyteller who'd gotten lost in the past.

Chapter Fourteen

1982

It wasn't till eleven that night that Mia returned home from wherever she'd been. Chuck had sent the girls to bed by eight—hours ago—and spent the rest of the time with a beer on the sofa, hardly remembering to sip it, his eyes on the window. Where could she be?

Chuck and Mia had been married in a very small ceremony just a few months ago, not long after Chuck had left Margaret for good. He still remembered how strange it had been for him to look out on their little group of wedding guests and realize that not one of them had been a member of his former life. Still, he'd been happy, or mostly happy, finally stepping into the light and acknowledging his true feelings. He'd really thought, *Now I can be honest with myself and everyone else.*

But ever since they'd married, Mia hadn't gone out without him, not even with girlfriends. She'd always told him what she was up to. Usually, her outside-the-house experiences had something to do with their daughters or with tending to the car or bills or the house.

Now, Mia's car turned onto the driveway. She cut the engine and the lights. Chuck remained seated on the sofa, his eyes on the dark front door. But Mia didn't even look at him when she entered, still in that sleek black dress and a pair of gold earrings. Her face was stern and all the more beautiful for it—like something porcelain, it was better not to touch it for fear of breaking it. Chuck stood and looked at her, searching his mind for something to say. But Mia went to the staircase and disappeared.

Chuck walked slowly, following her. From the landing, he watched as she checked in on both of the girls, making sure they were sleeping soundly. It was almost like she didn't trust Chuck to do what he'd said he would. Then she went to their bedroom and removed her dress. She didn't face him, not once. She was in his pajamas by the time he reached their bedroom and sat at the edge of the mattress. His tongue burned. He wanted her to tell him everything. He wanted her secrets.

"Mia?" His voice sounded tentative and weak.

But Mia was already walking down the hallway. He listened as she brushed her teeth and face, then collapsed on the pillow behind him to watch the shadows on the ceiling. When she returned, she cut the lights and crawled into bed beside him. Together, they lay in complete silence.

Just ask her where she was, he thought. *She's your wife. You're her husband. You have to be honest with each other.*

But Chuck realized he couldn't ask. He knew what she would throw back in his face. She'd say, *You did whatever you wanted for years. You had two families. I went along with it. Aren't I allowed to do what I want every now and again?*

She would have every right to say that.

Chuck's hands were clammy. He was suddenly terrified that she'd begun an affair. But why would she? He was right here! He was in love with her! He reached over and touched her shoulder, but she turned to her side, facing away from him. The signal was clear.

Chuck woke up the following morning in an empty bed. His first fear—that Mia had taken the children and left him—was squashed when he heard the sound of the eggs cooking in the skillet downstairs. His daughters were laughing about something. He rolled over to check the time. It was seven fifteen. He'd finally slept more than a few hours at a time. He'd needed it.

But downstairs, Mia didn't seem any more keen on talking to him than she'd been last night. She set a plate of eggs in front of him and turned around. Oriana and Meghan were either too clever to mention it or oblivious. Oriana started asking him questions about geography— which state capitals he remembered and so on. Chuck had a horrible headache. He wanted to go back to bed.

When Mia took the girls to school, Meghan and Oriana kissed him on the cheek and scrambled out the door. Mia didn't look at him. She shut the door between them, leaving Chuck to stew in his own sinister fears.

Chuck went to work until he got tired of it. He really felt like he was at the end of his rope job-wise. Sitting at a desk felt increasingly soulless. Didn't he have enough money? Hadn't he been working himself to the bone since he was sixteen years old? By three thirty, he was out the door and headed to the bar near the harbor, the one where most of the patrons were sailors or fishermen, there to warm up after spending heinous cold days on the sea. Although Chuck was wealthy with a prominent business, he appreciated these kinds of bars. Everyone mostly kept to themselves. They didn't really care about his money or his name; they weren't trying to impress him.

Chuck sat at the bar and ordered a beer. Storm clouds rolled over the island, shooting rain over the bar's tin roof. He sipped half of his beer and zoned out, thinking about Mia and his children.

But it wasn't long after that that he heard the name Roger Albright.

"The rumors about that man are outlandish, to say the least." This came from a rough-around-the-edges fisherman who looked like he'd already had too many beers. "You think it's likely his children killed him for his cash?"

"No doubt about it," another fisherman said. "That's what these wealthy types do. You bring them into the world, you teach them about money and how to love money, and then they kill you in pursuit of the very thing you've taught them to love above all else. It's Roger's own fault, is what it is."

"Kids are smart," another fisherman said. "They don't forget what they've learned."

Chuck's stomach roiled. What had he taught Grant and Roland? That it was okay to cheat on the woman you loved? That it was okay to wrong the woman who'd given birth to your children? Roland and Grant had both taken "hush" money and abandoned their relationship with their father forever. What did that mean about what kind of people they were?

Suddenly, the door burst open, bringing in a strong and sharp draft. Chuck stared into his beer. The bar quieted for a moment before the fishermen began chatting about Roger Albright again.

Chuck wondered if Vivian was still up at the hospital. He pondered if Travis was still dipping in to read and chat with her. Maybe Vivian had already sent him away, realizing how strange and lonely he was.

She was French, after all. She'd been on her way elsewhere—somewhere beautiful and warm and tropical. She wanted nothing to do with Martha's Vineyard or some lighthouse keeper's son.

A fist slammed on the bar beside Chuck. "I need a beer."

Chuck turned to find Clarence beside him. He was drunk and leaning from side to side. His face and hands were bright red. He hadn't yet noticed Chuck. Chuck's heart stopped. This was nobody he wanted to deal with right now. He considered sneaking out of there and heading back to the office.

"You sure you need another one, buddy?" the bartender asked Clarence. "Looks as though you've had enough."

Clarence scoffed. "I'm here, aren't I? My money is just as good as everyone else's, isn't it?"

The bartender rolled his eyes, turned around, and poured Clarence a beer. Chuck kept his eyes down. Maybe Clarence was too drunk to recognize him.

Clarence took a long drink of beer and smacked his lips. Chuck furrowed his brow and thought about the first time he'd seen Clarence—not even forty-eight hours ago.

And then, Clarence started talking.

"It isn't what I thought it would be, this life," he began. His eyes turned toward Chuck, pegging him. It was clear he knew who he was.

He wasn't too drunk to know that, at least.

Chuck's cheeks were red. He didn't know what to say.

"You wake up every day, and you do the best you can," Clarence continued. "You pray for the best if you're the praying type at all. And if you're not?" Clarence shrugged. "It's all the same."

Chuck filled his mouth with beer and searched the bar for someone to commiserate with. Everyone kept their eyes averted.

"Call me crazy, but I'm an old-fashioned man," Clarence continued. "I'm the sort of guy who says what he wants to do and does it. I don't like hiding things."

Chuck still didn't know what to say. Clearly, Clarence was out of his mind.

"What about you, Chuck?" Clarence demanded. "Are you the kind of guy who keeps his word?"

A terrible smile spread over Clarence's face. Chuck was genuinely terrified.

"No. Chuck Coleman isn't the kind of guy who keeps his word," Clarence answered his own question. "Are you, Chuck?"

"You're drunk, Clarence," Chuck said.

Clarence raised his finger. "I may be drunk, but I still know the truth. I've always known it." He continued to smile. "You know who else knows the truth?"

Chuck gave Clarence a narrow-eyed look. He had no idea what he was going on about.

"Mia knows the truth," Clarence finished.

Mia? My wife, Mia? Chuck thought. Rage filled his heart. He was suddenly out of his chair. He'd never punched anyone before and wouldn't start now. But his hands were in fists, and his ears rang with danger.

"What did you just say?"

Clarence continued to leer at him. He took another sip from his beer.

"Repeat yourself," Chuck demanded. "I dare you."

Chuck remembered that Mia had acted strangely when he'd mentioned the lighthouse keeper.

What did it mean? Chuck had assumed they knew each other; all islanders did. But this? This felt like something else. Something deeper.

Had Mia been with Clarence last night? It was impossible. In that sleek black dress, with those earrings? She wouldn't deign to sit at a table with Clarence, let alone do what adults did behind closed doors.

Mia wouldn't cheat on me. Would she?

But suddenly, Clarence's weight shifted. The chair fell back, and he collapsed across the hardwood of that dank dive bar. Chuck panicked. Everyone at the bar let out a cry of alarm.

"Should we call 911?" someone demanded from the corner.

The bartender and Chuck kneeled beside Clarence to check his vital signs.

"My guess is he's just drunk as a skunk," the bartender said. "He doesn't have insurance, either. He wouldn't like it if we called the ambulance. Who would pay for it?"

Chuck thought, *I would pay for it, but I wouldn't like it.*

But Clarence came to a moment later.

His eyes were strange, like those of a goldfish. Chuck felt a wave of compassion for him and took his hand in his to help him up. It was clear he was a raving drunk, that he was lonely, that he didn't know up from down or day from night. That should have been obvious when Chuck first met him on the beach the night of the accident. Clarence got on his knees and met Chuck's gaze. After a firm nod, he heaved himself the rest of the way to his feet. Chuck wrapped an arm around him, hurrying to keep him upright. Chuck swayed like a boat at sea.

"He can sleep it off in back," the bartender said, pointing a thumb behind him.

Chuck shook his head. "I'll get him home."

Chuck half carried and half led Clarence to his car, where he stuffed the massive man in the passenger seat. He tried to buckle him in, but he failed to.

"Where is Travis?" Chuck asked, turning the key to start the engine. "Is he at the lighthouse? The cabin?"

Clarence made a grunt that Chuck was pretty sure meant "lighthouse." After all, the night would be falling soon; somebody needed to be there to ensure the light shone across the sound.

Chuck drove to the lighthouse and parked out front. Clarence had fallen asleep on the ride, and he was snoring loudly, his head tipped back. He was much too heavy to carry up the stairs. But Chuck wasn't sure what to do. A part of him wanted to shake him and ask why he'd spoken about Mia like that. Another part of him didn't want to know.

Chuck got out of the car and entered the lighthouse, leaving Clarence asleep in his car. He felt lightheaded. When he reached the door at the top, he knocked. Travis answered a split second later, wearing a happy and curious smile.

"Chuck!" he said. "This is a surprise!"

He spoke as though Chuck and Travis had known one another for years rather than fewer than two days.

Travis bolted away from the door to tend to something near the window. This left Chuck to hang in the doorway, watching. Travis looked even more spry than he had when he'd first met him, his legs and arms long and lined with muscles. Did Travis know anything about Clarence's potential relationship with Mia? Would he sell out his father by telling him?

But before Chuck could get a word in about Mia or Clarence, Travis was already babbling about Vivian. "She's getting better by the hour, I swear," he said, working diligently on something in the corner. It looked as though he was trying to repair a radio. "And she's teaching me French! Je voudrais ecrivain." His accent was atrocious, but he smiled as he spoke the strange-to-him language. "Oh, but there was some drama at the hospital today," Travis said and twisted around to look at Chuck. Travis wanted to see what Chuck looked like when he said it. "Natasha disappeared."

"Natasha left?" Chuck was surprised at this. Vivian was her daughter; why would Natasha leave the hospital when Vivian was still bedridden?

"Remember how she was freaking out about Roger Albright's disappearance?" Travis asked, waving his screwdriver in the air.

Chuck raised his shoulders. "She could have been panicking about anything. She was just involved in a major accident."

"I think it's all related," Travis said.

"Has Vivian mentioned anything?" Chuck asked.

"She did talk about Roger," Travis said thoughtfully. "Very briefly. She asked if he'd been found yet. When I said he hadn't, she looked really worried. It made me wonder!"

"Wonder what, exactly?" Chuck was losing patience. He wanted to drag Clarence out of his car and pepper him with questions about Mia.

"I don't know," Travis said. "But Roger's four children over in Manhattan are certainly eager to get their inheritance. In the waiting room at the hospital, I learned that Roger divorced their mother recently. You don't think they'd take him out? For revenge?"

Again, Chuck thought of Roland and Grant. They'd taken his money as a sort of "revenge" after Chuck's affair. There was no end to what people would do.

Travis seemed on the verge of pestering Chuck with more questions and more information about this "case," which he'd seemingly decided to solve himself (despite not having much in the way of information). But Chuck interrupted him.

"I have your dad in my car," he said.

Travis's face transformed. He looked stricken. "Is he drunk?"

"As a skunk," Chuck said.

Travis tugged his hair and glanced back at the ocean. It was late afternoon, and light had begun to dim, casting it in dark turquoise and navy blues. "We'd better hurry," he said. "I'll help you."

Chuck and Travis went downstairs to find Clarence bleary-eyed and mumbling in Chuck's car. It was clear he wasn't sure where he was. But as soon as they hauled him out, Clarence tipped his head back and took stock of the gorgeous lighthouse, the place he'd pledged to maintain.

"Here she is," he said of the lighthouse. "My pride and joy."

It wasn't as difficult to get Clarence up the stairs as Chuck had expected. It was as though Clarence found another level of strength within himself. He shot up the stairs, leaving Chuck and Travis in his wake, howling the entire way.

Travis turned back and looked at Chuck. "Thanks for bringing him in. He gets this way when he has days off. But it's like he said already. This job is lonely. He doesn't always know what to do with his thoughts."

Chuck bowed his head. "I understand," he said.

He headed back home after that, eager to see Mia and ask her about Clarence. But the minute he entered his house, she hurried past him, calling behind her, "I'm heading out for the night."

Chuck found himself home alone with the girls again. He wondered if he'd permanently destroyed his own happiness. He wondered if he'd had it coming.

Chapter Fifteen

Present Day

It was the week after Estelle's Christmas-cookie-decorating party and just a couple of weeks till Christmas. Like always during the morning—regardless of the season—Estelle found herself at her desk, typing notes for her lighthouse keeper romance. But the note-taking was slow going. For whatever reason, every time she tried to delve into the romance of her fictional story, her mind tugged her back to thoughts of the sunken ship, Vivian Knight in her wheelchair in Martha's Vineyard, and why Chuck was so dang curious about an incident that had happened more than forty years ago. It was all stranger than fiction. What was he hiding? And why did it seem as though Estelle was the last person on earth who cared about it?

Feeling all over the place and unfocused, Estelle called Sam to see what she was up to.

"Darcy and I were just about to grab brunch! You want to come?" Sam sounded happy. "It's freezing outside, but the snow is gorgeous. It's nice to be downtown."

Estelle was already on her feet. "I'll be there in fifteen minutes!"

"We'll be here!" Sam cried.

Estelle hurried, pulling on jeans and a sweater and running out the door. Roland was off with Grant somewhere. He'd told her what they were up to, but she'd filed it somewhere in her mind, somewhere she couldn't get to right now. She drove slowly, her hands at ten and two as she moved through the snowy island and parked in the lot behind the brunch spot.

Darcy and Sam were seated at the window booth, aglow from the snowy light. Estelle bent to hug them both.

"Look at the photo Rachelle just sent!" Darcy cried, pulling up an image of Rachelle next to the Mediterranean Sea with a big plate of pasta in front of her. "She's on vacation on an island near Rome."

"That's our girl!" Estelle cried. "When should we visit her? You've already been, but I haven't!"

Darcy sighed and glanced down at her stomach—proof that she probably wouldn't manage to leave the country anytime soon, proof that nothing in her life would ever be free and easy again. Estelle hesitated. She hoped she hadn't said something wrong.

The server arrived to take their order. Estelle went with green tea and a vegetarian omelet with feta cheese. Sam ordered bacon and eggs, while Darcy opted for avocado toast.

"So," Darcy said, smiling as she changed the subject, "are you still looking into your sunken ship?"

Estelle smiled. "I can't get enough of it. But I'm not the best researcher in the world."

"I've been wondering about the fifth Albright heir," Sam said, wrapping both hands around her cup of coffee. "Is there a way you can figure out who that might be?"

"There has to be a list somewhere of who was on that ship," Darcy agreed. "Police records, maybe?"

Sam nodded furiously. Warmth spread through Estelle's arms and legs. She considered telling them that she needed to find Travis, too—the husband of the woman who lived down the hall from Chuck. But she wasn't entirely sure why he wanted to know, and she didn't want to give him away.

"I'd dig deeper into what happened immediately after the shipwreck, too," Darcy said. "Maybe there were legal battles between the Albright siblings? Maybe something came to the surface and was immediately scrubbed out again?"

Estelle took her notebook from her purse and hurriedly wrote down Darcy's ideas. She met her grand-daughter's gaze over the table and said, "You're good at this. Why didn't you ever get into research?"

But Darcy waved her hands. "I just figured out my calling," she explained, speaking of her new gig with Reese and Joel and their app development company. "I don't want to distract myself with another career idea."

Estelle laughed. "It's too bad we can't live numerous lives, isn't it? Maybe I would have followed several other paths just to see where they led me."

"But being a writer was what you were always meant to do," Sam said.

Estelle beamed over her steaming green tea. She had another direction. She couldn't wait to dig further.

After brunch, Estelle drove out to the harbor and onto the ferry. It was winter, and the boat went between Martha's Vineyard and Nantucket at odd times, but it didn't always make it back when the schedule said it would. After she parked, she called Roland to tell him she was "following a lead." He didn't answer, so she left a voice message and said there was leftover chili in the freezer. All he had to do was heat it in the microwave—if he didn't eat with Grant, which he often did when they spent their days together.

Estelle returned to the Martha's Vineyard Historical Society by three thirty that afternoon. Amy was there, just as she'd been last time, and she greeted Estelle warmly and said, "The place is all yours again! Nobody ever comes in here anymore. It's like everyone has given up on the past." Estelle thanked her and decided to be open about her task. Maybe Amy would throw herself into helping her.

"I would love to find a list of everyone on board the shipwreck of October 1982," Estelle said, clasping her hands. "Is that something you'd have here?"

Amy's eyes were illuminated. Without answering, she hurried over to the dusty computer and began to type furiously. Then, like a dog who'd caught a scent, she pointed herself toward the corner of the room and sped off. Estelle was hot on her heels.

It didn't take long for Amy to find the old newspaper clipping within which the journalist listed every person— alive or dead—who'd been aboard the cruise ship the night it sank. Amy passed over the laminated page with a happy smile.

"Thank you," Estelle said, eyeing the list, which now seemed overly long. "I appreciate it."

"Let me know if you need anything else."

Estelle sat with the list of survivors and victims of the shipwreck of 1982. It didn't take long to find Vivian Morceau's name; she was the youngest person aboard the vessel the night it sank. She was also the young woman at the retirement facility. But what did strike Estelle as odd was this: Vivian wasn't the only Morceau aboard the vessel that night. There was another Morceau. Natasha Morceau. Was she Vivian's sister? Mother? Cousin?

Estelle hurried back to the computer to type "Natasha Morceau" into the database. Unfortunately, the only articles that came up were Martha's Vineyard-based and related to the sunken ship. None of them listed anything about Natasha save for the fact that she'd survived the wreck. They didn't even show a photograph or an age.

Was there another way to learn more about Natasha?

Estelle took to Google for answers.

In the soft light of the historical society, she went through page after page of Google articles, praying for an answer about who Natasha was and where she might be now. At the worst, this was a dead end. But Estelle had a strange inkling about Natasha. She couldn't help but think that Natasha Morceau was Roger Albright's lover— and the mother of Vivian Morceau.

She wasn't sure where this idea came from. It was a "hunch" in the truest form.

But Estelle had been around forever. She'd studied people. More than that, she'd studied Chuck, who'd had a mistress, too. His mistress had given birth to his second family.

Maybe Roger Albright and Chuck Coleman had that in common.

These stories were incredibly common among successful and wealthy men Estelle knew.

Maybe that's why Chuck was so curious about Vivian in the first place.

It took Estelle nearly two hours of searching through newspaper databases and historical Reddit threads to discover something of value.

The headline read: SHIPWRECK SURVIVOR SUES ALBRIGHT CHILDREN.

Estelle nearly jumped out of her chair. She clicked through the article to find a photograph of a woman in her forties, maybe. She was seated in a courtroom and was sensationally pretty but volatile-looking. The article was brief. It said, rather simply, that Natasha Morceau had sued the Albright children to include herself and her daughter Vivian as heirs to Roger Albright's estate. Natasha stipulated that Roger was poised to marry Natasha and put her and Vivian in his will. More than that, she suggested that Vivian was Roger's legal heir, who had been born after Natasha and Roger had an affair eighteen years ago.

At the time of Natasha suing the Albright children, Roger had still been deemed "missing." The judge suggested that Roger had gone into hiding to avoid dealing with "all the people after his money." He dismissed Natasha. He said it was clear she was a "hungry home-wrecker." Her assertion that Vivian was Roger's real daughter was basically laughed out of court.

As Estelle read, her blood boiled for Natasha and for Vivian. She didn't know these women; she didn't know their personalities, how they operated, or whether or not they were the sorts of women who wanted to take advantage of billionaires who'd gone missing. But she also knew what it was like to be a woman in the world. She knew what it was like to be laughed at and called "crazy." It frequently happened to her as a female writer—especially among male writers who deemed themselves more worthy of accolades.

She wasn't sure why, but she believed Natasha. Even forty-two years later.

Amy approached with a small bag of salt and vinegar chips.

"You've been hard at work all day," Amy said proudly.

Estelle took two chips and furrowed her brow.

"It's for a book, right?" Amy asked.

Estelle turned to look at Amy, surprised that Amy had recognized her.

"I've read five of your books," Amy said with a smile. "Who doesn't love your books?"

Estelle smiled and thanked her. Amy left the bag of chips behind and went back to her computer. As her fingers tapped out a rhythm, Estelle suddenly found herself with an idea.

Who doesn't love your books? Amy had asked.

Was it possible one of the Albright children loved her books, too?

Estelle grabbed her phone and wrote an email to her agent, asking if she could set up an interview with one of the Albright children—preferably one of Roger Albright's daughters. They were around her age, after all. If Estelle was lucky, the women were fans.

Estelle left the Martha's Vineyard Historical Society and headed back to her car. Winter sun glowed from behind thick snow-filled clouds.

When she got into her car, her agent called. "What's this about?" She sounded chipper and confused.

"I'm researching for my lighthouse keeper romance," Estelle said, keeping her voice even.

"Why do you need to talk to a billionaire's child to learn more about a lighthouse keeper?" her agent asked.

Estelle laughed. She had to keep things light. "You have connections, don't you?"

"I have a million and a half connections," her agent said with a sigh. "I've already checked on it. It looks like Penelope Albright published a book with your publisher just last year. A women's fiction novel that didn't sell very well."

Estelle's ears rang.

"I'll contact your editor and see if we can set up a meeting," her agent said. "How does that sound?"

"It sounds like you're a dream agent," Estelle said.

Her agent laughed. "Don't flatter me. Just get that book to me soon! I'm eager for a spring-time sale."

Estelle smiled. "I'll see what I can do."

Instead of heading immediately back to the ferry, Estelle drove to Chuck's retirement home. It had been a little while since they'd talked. As a gift, she'd printed out the wedding announcement and photograph for Vivian and Travis. She wanted him to know she was working on learning more.

Chuck was in his chair with another documentary on television. This one was about China. He lent Estelle a somber smile and took the newspaper clipping and photograph with both hands. His expression was difficult to read.

"They were just kids," he said finally.

Estelle sat down across from him and crossed her legs. She shivered.

"I knew he fell in love with her after the accident," Chuck said, palming the back of his neck. "He was out of his mind for her, always going to the hospital to see if she was all right. But I lost touch with him and his father shortly after that."

Estelle's heart burned to know more. "You were close with Clarence and Travis?"

"Not really," Chuck said. He gave her a look Estelle meant to mean: I don't trust anyone with this story, not even you.

Estelle wondered if she should give him more. Maybe then, he'd trust her.

"You know the cruise ship belonged to Roger Albright?" Estelle said. "Roger Albright was said to have died that night. After that, his four children got millions upon millions of dollars."

Chuck shook his head vaguely. "Right."

"But did you also know that it was rumored that Roger Albright had a fifth child?" Estelle said. She pulled up the result she'd found via Google—an old clipping from when Natasha Morceau had tried to sue the Albright children. Chuck took the phone and furrowed his brow at the screen. Finally, he reached for his reading glasses and fully took in what it meant.

Chuck's lips parted with surprise. "Goodness," he said.

It was clear he hadn't had this information before.

"There were whispers of foul play," he said after a long time. "But do you really think the Albright children tried to take out their father, his mistress, and their daughter in one fell swoop?"

Estelle raised her eyebrows. "That's what I'm trying to figure out."

Chuck handed the phone back to her. He looked grave with worry. "I'd be careful, Estelle. These people are powerful."

Estelle promised she would be.

"No news on where Travis is?" Chuck asked a bit later as she buttoned her coat and prepared to go. "I see Vivian every day, all by herself. She never has any visitors. I sit with her, but she doesn't even look at me. It tears me up inside, thinking that she's by herself in this world."

Estelle grimaced. "I'm still looking for Travis," she lied, although she'd sort of lost track of Travis in the chaos of everything else. "But remember that Vivian isn't alone. You're here with her. After all these years."

Chuck said goodbye with a dull voice. Estelle glanced back at him, where he sat in quiet contemplation, before she ducked down the hallway and headed back to her car. After another several inches of snow, the ferries had closed for the evening. It meant she was headed back to Margorie Tomlinson's for a cozy night of wine and conversation.

By the time she pulled into Margorie's driveway, her agent had messaged her back: You have a meeting with Penelope Albright next week.

Estelle doubted she'd be able to sleep tonight.

Chapter Sixteen

It was the morning after Estelle's surprise visit. Chuck woke up at six thirty with a nervous energy. It felt as though he'd dreamed about sinking ships and dark water, about screaming French women and lost souls. Trying to dig his way out of it, he did his stretching routine, then showered, got dressed, and went to the dining room for oatmeal and coffee. A few of his friends were already there, up and chatting about their families, about Christmas "just around the corner." A massive Christmas tree sat in the center of the dining room, its star scraping the ceiling. It reminded Chuck of that film *Christmas Vacation.* Although when he'd said that to Bethany once, she'd said, "That movie is not funny at all! It's an insult to Christmas!"

But Chuck found it difficult to slide into conversation with his friends. His voice sounded false.

"Your family will come get you for Christmas, won't they?" Dan asked as he spooned oatmeal from his bowl.

"They won't give me a moment to myself," Chuck tried to joke.

A few people at his table didn't laugh. Chuck immediately regretted his joke. After all, not everyone had the tremendous family he had. Not everyone had people to spend Christmas with.

Some people couldn't even afford the retirement facility in the first place. His heart ached for those lost souls.

In his pocket, he had the print-out of Vivian and Travis's wedding announcement, and he took it out frequently over coffee, looking at those youthful faces. Back in the eighties, Chuck had been in his fifties; he'd thought he was old. But there was still so much joy and heartache awaiting him. Decades of it.

"What's that, Chuck?" Dan asked.

Chuck folded the newspaper clipping and put it back in his pocket. "Nothing much. Just something I don't want to forget." He tapped his forehead. It was common for older people to forget things easily. But Chuck—mercifully or not—remembered almost everything.

Dan laughed. "I have to write everything down, too! That's old age for you."

Chuck smiled. It was nice to pretend. He wondered if Dan was pretending, too.

Two hours after breakfast, Oriana and Meghan swung by with more Christmas decorations for Chuck's suite—plus a platter of homemade cookies, which Oriana and her daughter, Alexis, had baked yesterday evening. Apparently, toddler Benny had helped, too, and spilled flour and sugar all over the kitchen floor. Oriana showed pictures of the wreckage, and Chuck laughed appreciatively. "He's a boy after my own heart," he said.

By that, Chuck meant *he makes messes, like me.*

"We made lemon bars! Your favorite!" Oriana said,

unfurling the plastic wrap from the top of the platter. "And Christmas cut-outs and buckeyes and peanut butter blossoms." She smiled, pleased with herself.

Meghan had already started stringing lights and tinsel around Chuck's room. Chuck remained in his chair, nibbling a lemon bar and watching his daughter's work. Because it mattered to him and to them, he pestered them about their careers—Oriana's art deals and Meghan's trading, a job he'd taught her himself. They talked about the difficulties of working for themselves, which Chuck understood well, having been a longtime entrepreneur and business owner.

Suddenly, Chuck asked a question that seemed to come out of nowhere. He hadn't even realized he was going to ask it until it flew out of his mouth.

"Do you remember that I wasn't around very much when you were little?"

Meghan dropped the tinsel and turned to face him. Oriana was trying to open a cardboard box and furrowed her brow.

"You know the story," Chuck offered. His face was getting hotter by the second. "You know that I was trying to live two lives at once."

Meghan's cheek twitched. It was clear that neither of them wanted to discuss this.

"I'm just curious if you remember me not being around," he said, backing himself in a corner. "Do you resent me for it?"

Oriana's shoulders sagged. She looked frightened, as though she thought he'd lost his mind.

"Dad, we don't blame you," Oriana breathed, reaching for his hand.

Meghan hurried up to the other side of the armchair. "It was a long time ago."

"But we have so many memories of you," Oriana said. "You taught us everything we know."

"Your mother taught you the important things," Chuck reminded them. "She taught you to be honest and kind." He folded his lips and muttered, "I hope I taught you to care about more than just money. It's all I used to care about. And I think I poisoned half the Colemans because of it."

Meghan bent down beside him. She was the calmer of his two daughters; she didn't fly off the handle the way Oriana sometimes did.

"Don't talk yourself into that narrative," she said softly. "You taught us how to love. You taught us how to pass that love onto our families. You are a strong and wonderful father. Please, don't forget that."

Chuck's heart shattered. He fell silent and allowed his daughters to continue their work, decorating his little suite with more Christmas flair than any man could ever need. Frequently, he spotted them exchanging worried glances. He knew they'd have numerous conversations later, telling each other he'd just gotten so old.

For lunch, Roland and Grant swung by the retirement facility. It was a surprise, although Chuck worried it was all because of his "panic moment." Maybe his daughters had called his sons to come make sure their father was all right. But his sons brought no air of worry. Instead, the five of them sat in the dining room and swapped old stories, sharing food and laughing together as snow swirled outside.

Toward the end of lunch, Grant was in heavy conversation with Meghan, and Oriana got up to use the bathroom. It left Chuck "alone" with Roland, his eldest.

He still remembered the exhilarating magic of holding his firstborn in his arms for the first time.

He blinked tears out of his eyes.

"Did Estelle mention she stopped by a few times?" Chuck asked.

"She did," Roland said. "She's heavily researching her next novel. It seems like you've seen her more than me." He laughed. "I love it when she gets so immersed. Chasing a story is like magic for her."

Chuck tilted his head. He wondered how much of the story Estelle had told Roland. Had she asked him, *Why is your father so obsessed with this shipwreck?*

But she was obsessed, too.

Midafternoon, Roland, Grant, Meghan, and Oriana left the retirement facility, citing things they had to take care of at home and at the store and online and elsewhere. *When you're young, there's so much to do*, Chuck thought. They hugged their father and promised they'd be back soon. Chuck waved goodbye and headed back to his room, worried that the immensity of the Christmas decorations would depress him.

Chuck took the long way back to his suite. He waved to Claire, who was wheeling a guy even older than Chuck through the halls. He even stopped at the front desk to wish everyone a happy afternoon. But the woman behind the counter—one with another ridiculous Santa hat—spoke to him in an overly bubbly voice, one that reminded him that people younger than him no longer respected him, not now that he was so gosh-darn old. It depressed him.

Chuck walked toward the room with the large television to see what was on. Like always, at this time of the year, they were showing Christmas films. He didn't recognize this one, but the main character was beautiful, and the love interest was handsome, and there was no doubt they'd get together by the end of the movie. *Life isn't really like that,* he wanted to remind everyone watching the film. But we all knew that, didn't we? We were all in our eighties and nineties. We'd lived our lives. We'd said goodbye to our houses. Many of us had buried our spouses. Our "Christmas romances" were long behind us.

Suddenly, he spotted Vivian Knight. As ever, she was in her wheelchair, tucked off in the corner but pointed toward the television. Chuck's heart seized. He touched the photograph of her he had in his pocket and steeled himself for disappointment. But he had to try to make a connection. Slowly, he walked behind the sofas and big cushioned chairs, making his way over to Vivian. Once there, he pulled up a chair to sit directly beside her. Not five feet to his left was a woman in her eighties—a woman wearing a beautiful maroon dress, her hair styled in glossy white curls. Chuck felt her sidelong glance.

Who was she? Chuck didn't recognize her.

But he was here to talk to Vivian.

"Hi, Vivian," he said quietly, not wanting to bother anyone watching the film. "I don't know if you remember me, but I remember you." He pulled the photo the rest of the way out of his pocket and spread it out across his thigh.

Vivian still didn't look at him. It felt akin to being ignored by a much younger woman.

Chuck knew she wasn't all there. But he still felt embarrassed.

"My daughter-in-law printed this photo out for me,"

he said, lifting it so Vivian could "see" it. "It's you and Travis on your wedding day in the eighties! Look at you. You must be nineteen years old?" His heart felt on the verge of breaking. He turned to look at Vivian's eyes.

His stupid hope was that she would see the photograph and immediately be able to speak again. He'd hoped she would say, "Oh, my love, Travis!" and then launch into an explanation about Roger Albright and her mother and what had happened since that fateful night in 1982.

It was a night that had brought together so many lost souls.

But it did seem as though Vivian was looking at the photograph. Her brow was furrowed, and she had her hands stretched over her thighs. She looked painfully beautiful and tragic.

"This is your husband," Chuck continued softly. "Where is he? Who brought you here, Vivian?"

Why are you all alone? You're too young to be all alone!

Suddenly, the woman in the maroon dress turned to look at him. Her eyes were like a cat's. Slowly, he set his photograph back on his lap and looked at her. Vivian didn't seem to notice. She continued to watch the television ahead of her as though nothing had happened.

Chuck thought he was going to burst into tears.

As quickly as his bones could take him, he got to his feet and stumbled toward the hall. He touched the wall and gasped for breath.

"Excuse me?" a woman's voice rang out.

Chuck wanted to escape it. He wanted to go to his suite, close the door behind him, and block out the world. The world was a cruel and unusual place. It had destroyed Vivian's youth and vitality. It had killed her memory. It had taken Travis away.

"Chuck?"

At the sound of his name, Chuck froze. The woman in the maroon dress circled him and faced him. Her face was etched with worry.

Why did she know his name? Why didn't he know hers?

Noting his confusion, the woman touched her chest and said, "It's Sylvia Morrow."

Chuck's heart lifted. "Sylvia. Of course." He'd met her twenty years ago during a coastal hike—he was seventy-something, and she in her sixties. At the time, she'd been married to Sil Morrow. She'd told him she liked going on hikes by herself. She'd told him, *I don't have to pretend to be anyone but myself or to think anything that I don't want to think or make conversation if I don't feel like it. It's just me and the birds.*

But right now, Chuck saw no wedding band on her finger. Divorce? Death?

Anything might have happened over the past twenty years.

"It's good to see you," Chuck stuttered, feeling foolish. "I'm sorry. I didn't recognize you at first."

"It's because I got old," Sylvia said with a cackle.

"We're lucky," Chuck said. "Some people never got the chance to get old."

Sylvia nodded. "I think about that all the time." Her eyes danced. "Do you know Mrs. Knight?"

Chuck still had the photograph of Vivian and Travis in his hand. He held it up and showed it to Sylvia because he couldn't think of anything else to do.

Sylvia took it and looked at it for a long time. "She was such a beautiful girl."

Chuck was sure that Sylvia had been, too. But looks mattered so little. They went away so quickly.

"I knew her husband," Chuck explained stupidly. "And I met her back in the eighties when she was a teenager. It's broken my heart to see her in that chair every day. I can't imagine what happened." He swallowed. "She hit her head when she was younger. She was in a coma briefly. I can't help but wonder if that has something to do with why she can't talk."

Sylvia grimaced. "Those kinds of things have a way of catching up to us, don't they?"

Chuck sighed.

Sylvia reached out and touched his shoulder. It felt so soft and gentle. Chuck blinked to keep from crying. *What's gotten into me? Why am I such a sap?*

"Chuck? Do you like tea?" Sylvia asked.

Chuck felt the corners of his lips pull up. "I do."

"Would you like to have some tea with me?"

It was the only thing in the world Chuck wanted to do right then.

Chapter Seventeen

Estelle was too jittery to let anyone else drive to Manhattan.

"Why don't you let me take the wheel for a while?" Sam suggested on the ferry between Nantucket and Hyannis, adjusting her winter hat on her head as Darcy, Aria, and Hilary grabbed tea from the little coffee shop aboard the vessel. Snow whirred down on the other side of the window, dramatic and thick, and the ocean looked frothy and not at all welcoming. It was hard to believe that this was the same ocean in which Estelle had swum every day all summer long, grabbing sweet release as a big, beautiful sun beat down upon her island.

"Don't worry about it," Estelle said, giving her daughter a look that meant don't ask again. "I want to focus on the big interview. Driving helps."

Sam raised her shoulders. Darcy waddled over with a big smile and two teas, one of which she handed to her mother. Her eyes were electric. "Thanks again for the invitation, Grandma," she said. "The city is so magical at Christmastime."

Hilary bounded up with a big smile. Estelle guessed she was dieting heavily for her upcoming wedding, which meant very few Christmas cookies and very few glasses of wine. But Hilary was effervescent with joy.

"It's rare that Mom lets us into her writing world," she said of Estelle, her eyes on her.

Estelle waved her gloved hand.

But it was true that she was surprised she'd invited her daughters and granddaughters along for the ride at all. (Of course, she'd passed the invite on to Charlie's wife and daughters, but they hadn't been available.) She wondered why she'd done it. Did it speak to a general fear she had around meeting Penelope Albright? Did it speak to her inability to travel such a long distance by herself?

No, she realized now.

The reason she'd invited her daughters and theirs, she decided, was because of the story of Natasha and Vivian. She wanted to keep her loved ones close. She wanted them to know just how dear they were to her.

And she'd imagined them strolling the sunny snow-capped streets of Manhattan, gossiping and laughing, lost in the beauty of their surroundings and the love they had for each other.

The horn blew shortly thereafter. There was an announcement. "Please return to your vehicles. We'll soon be in Hyannis Port."

Estelle led her little squad downstairs and back to Sam's SUV, which was big enough for the five of them to sit comfortably. Estelle clambered in front and turned on the heat as Darcy got comfortable in the middle seat by herself. Because of her pregnancy, it was decided that the other three would cram in the back. Darcy glowed and rubbed her hands together.

"Remember, I'm happy sitting in a coffee shop downtown and watching pedestrians go by," Darcy said of their upcoming trip. "I don't want to hold anyone back from shopping the entire day away!"

"You won't hold us back, Darcy," Aria said with a smile. "You'll be our homebase."

"Exactly," Hilary declared. "After I drive myself crazy at the makeup counter, I'll come cry to you over a little dessert and a cappuccino."

"It's a deal." Darcy beamed.

The ferry creaking against the concrete side activated Estelle's anxiety. With her hands on ten and two, she drove them carefully down the ferry ramp and out of the harbor. The snow continued to whirl, but Sam's windshield wipers worked sensationally well, and the other drivers on the road were driving safer than usual. Nobody wanted an accident this close to Christmas.

The entire five-hour drive went by without a hitch. Estelle was so nervous about approaching the meeting with Penelope Albright that she decided to go slower. She half prayed for a traffic jam just to give herself a little more time to think and breathe. But before she knew it, she drove through skyscrapers as Darcy, Aria, Sam, and Hilary took photographs of snowy Manhattan, oohing and aahing about how sensational it looked.

Estelle had booked their rooms in the iconic Lucerne Hotel near Central Park on the Upper West Side. After a quick exchange with a valet driver, she handed over Sam's keys and led them into the lobby. Just like the last time she was here, the receptionist recognized her. "Estelle Coleman! Welcome back. I'm so pleased to be the one to welcome you."

Estelle felt her granddaughters' gazes and felt a jolt of

pride. Once, Sam had told Estelle what an inspiration Estelle was. She'd said, "Women your age don't often go after their dreams anymore. I love that my daughters can look at you and realize it's never too late." Estelle's heart had swelled. She'd thought, *I want my granddaughters to know that age is just a number.*

She imagined they were thinking it now, too.

The receptionist handed them key cards and asked the bellhops to take their suitcases up to their tenth-floor suites. One was for Aria and Hilary, another was for Sam and Darcy, and the final was for Estelle, who needed space and quiet to write.

"Are you off for your meeting?" Sam asked Estelle right before she ducked inside and closed the door behind her.

"I'll leave in about a half hour," Estelle said, checking her phone for the time.

"Good luck," Sam said. "Let me know if you need anything?"

Estelle smiled. She hadn't yet explained the specifics of her meeting with Penelope Albright to Darcy or Sam, probably because of how nervous she was. The minute she mentioned "Albright" to Darcy, she knew Darcy would be out of her mind with excitement, peppering Estelle with questions about the Albright fortune and the fifth heir.

Vivian Morceau.

Estelle entered her suite and freshened up before her departure. Looking at herself in the mirror, she fixed her makeup, added blush, and fine-tuned her eyebrows. Right before she finished, she checked the jacket of her novel—the one that had sold international rights in Paris—to see if she resembled the author photo inside it. According to her agent, Penelope Albright had asked that Estelle bring a copy of this novel and autograph it for her. The photo had been taken five years ago. Now, Estelle looked the same but slightly older. Her hair was the same dyed color. Her eyes were lined and big.

Estelle packed her purse with the novel, donned her winter coat, hat, and gloves, and took the elevator downstairs. Although she'd initially envisioned herself in a cab, pumping herself up for her big discussion with Penelope, she'd been surprised to learn that Penelope's gorgeous penthouse apartment was just two blocks from the hotel. She could walk.

Estelle paused at the street corner, waiting for the light to change. Something caught her eye. She turned to see Darcy, Aria, Hilary, and Sam just three blocks away, moving together happily, smiling at the Christmas decorations. It was bizarre to see them all together like this and not be among them. Estelle yearned to run after them and join their Christmassy party.

But she had a job to do.

En route to Penelope's home, Estelle wondered how this "research" might play out in the novel she wanted to write about the lighthouse keeper and his love. Maybe she was too far from the narrative.

Perhaps she was doing all of this out of curiosity.

Maybe she was doing it out of a love for humanity.

She'd never known Natasha or Vivian. But based on what Chuck had told her about them, she knew that Natasha had nearly lost Vivian during the shipwreck.

Now, Vivian was all alone in that retirement facility, eyes vacant and staring at Christmas movie after Christmas movie.

It didn't seem right.

Were the Albright children to blame?

Estelle found herself at the front door of an old-world apartment building. The doorman wore a traditional brown two-piece outfit and looked at her with kind eyes lined with wrinkles.

"Good afternoon, Madame," he said.

"Hello. I'm here to see Penelope Albright," Estelle said, grateful that her voice didn't waver.

"You're Estelle? The writer?"

Estelle was surprised that he knew she was coming. Clearly, Penelope or a member of her staff had reported it to him.

The doorman let her inside and gave her instructions on how to reach the elevator. Estelle found it easily and stepped inside to find an elevator operator wearing an old-fashioned outfit.

"Albright?" The elevator operator smiled to show false teeth.

"Thank you," Estelle said, stepping inside. She could hardly breathe as the elevator went up and up and up to the top.

Estelle had never considered herself a con artist. But wasn't she here on false pretenses?

Her stomach roiled with fear.

But suddenly, the elevator doors opened right into Penelope Albright's multimillion-dollar apartment. Of the place, Estelle thought darkly, *Some of this money should have been Vivian's. You wouldn't have missed it.*

She stepped into the marble foyer as the elevator doors closed behind her. Penelope appeared a moment later. She wore a linen outfit and a silk robe that swept out behind her beautifully, and her face was clean and pore-less. On her lips, she wore the most incredible color of lipstick Estelle had ever seen. She wasn't sure if she'd ever seen anyone with that specific shade of dark red. Maybe it was a signature color that Penelope had made especially for her.

Penelope greeted her. "Estelle Coleman! What a pleasure it is." Her voice was like a song.

Estelle reached out to shake Penelope's hand, but Penelope breezed forward and kissed her on both cheeks instead as though she were French.

"The pleasure is mine," Estelle said, smiling. Her cheeks already hurt. "This is a gorgeous apartment."

"You really think? I'm not entirely sure. I've been here for decades, darling, and I still can't decide if I want to move to the other side of the park. I'm frozen with indecision!" Penelope giggled and led Estelle deeper into the apartment, into a sunken living room with ornate couches and antique furniture. Estelle wondered if Penelope had taken this furniture from her father after his death.

A Siamese cat sat on a cushion in the corner and glared at Estelle.

It was almost as though the cat knew what Estelle was up to. It seemed to say, *You're a snake. I'm watching you.*

"You can't imagine how excited I was to hear you wanted to interview me," Penelope said, reaching for a bottle of wine to pour them both glasses.

Estelle didn't like to drink this early in the day, and she certainly didn't want to get sloppy during this fake interview. But she accepted the drink, clinked glasses, and let her lips touch the liquid. Penelope didn't seem to notice her lack of interest in the drink.

Maybe I should have been a spy! Estelle thought, smiling at how silly she felt.

Penelope sat down on the sofa next to the cat and

stroked the beautiful creature. Estelle searched the living room for some sign of Penelope's husband, who, it was rumored, usually lived in Barcelona. Estelle wondered why. Did they not get along?

"I mean, I'm such a fan of yours," Penelope said.

"I'm a fan of yours, too," Estelle lied. "I read your book in a single day!"

Penelope gasped. "Estelle Coleman read my book? I can't believe it!" But her eyes were alight in a way that suggested she believed it. She assumed everyone loved her. She expected everyone loved what she did. Perhaps news of the low sales of her book had bounced off her. Maybe her employees hadn't even bothered to tell her.

She had so much money anyway. It didn't matter.

Estelle pulled her own novel out of her bag and passed it over to Penelope, who gushed, "I'm so glad they told you what I really wanted! A signed copy!" Estelle watched Penelope read what she'd written: "To Penelope, a true talent and a kindred spirit. Yours, Estelle." Penelope looked up, her eyes filled with tears.

She's a brilliant faker, Estelle thought. *But so am I!*

It was likely that Penelope had lied so much in her life that she struggled to know what the truth was at all.

Estelle knew she needed to be careful. She couldn't jump immediately into the lion's den. She removed her notebook and her cell phone and smiled. "I really appreciate you doing this for me."

Penelope swept her hand over her cat. "Who is my character, exactly?" Penelope asked, smiling. "My agent said you're modeling her after me. But what's her narrative?"

"She's a complicated woman. She's been through a great deal in her life," Estelle said delicately, turning on

154

the voice recorder on her phone. Sam had shown her how to operate it earlier that week.

Penelope nodded and furrowed her brow. It was clear that she thought she was complicated, too. "Yes," she said with an ironic laugh. "That sounds about right."

"Generally, the public has a different perception of her," Estelle said, spoon-feeding Penelope what she wanted to hear. "They think, because of her father, she's been handed everything on a silver platter."

Penelope scoffed. "It's not true."

"Exactly," Estelle said, clicking her pen and writing a bunch of gibberish on her pad. If Penelope asked about it, Estelle would lie and say her handwriting was impossible to read. "But that's why I wanted to talk to you in person. I need to know more about you as a woman. What's behind that gorgeous face and this sensational apartment? What's behind your award-winning novel? Who is Penelope Albright?"

Penelope looked like she might melt with happiness. "I'll tell you who Penelope Albright is," she said. "She's a woman who's pushed herself through every conceivable limitation. She's a heartbroken woman who's lost so much. She's..."

Estelle remained focused, making random notes to herself as Penelope talked on and on. Estelle decided to let her go for nearly forty minutes without interruption. Only once did she stop so she could refill a glass with wine. The cat stared at Estelle as though it dared her to make one false move.

But Estelle was ready when the time came.

Penelope had just hit on the subject of her mother. "When Mom passed away, that really forced me to reckon with who we'd been to one another." Penelope's eyes went to the window. "I don't know if any of this should go in your book..."

Estelle waved her hand. "You'll have a final say on the book. Don't worry."

Penelope nodded. "My mother and I went many years without talking. We grew so angry with one another. Once, she threw a vase at my head. It smashed into a million pieces. It cost twenty-five thousand dollars!" She laughed wryly. But then silence fell between them. Maybe Penelope was lost in thought, thinking about the cruelty of her mother, of that vase across the floor.

Estelle's stomach churned. "How old were you when your mother and father got divorced?"

"I was an adult," Penelope said. "But it still ripped me apart. My father wasn't always a very kind man. I knew he'd really hurt my mother. He'd gone behind her back."

"He'd had an affair?" Estelle asked. In her mind's eye, she pictured Natasha Morceau. Would Penelope know her name if she brought it up?

"Rich and powerful men always have affairs," Penelope said as though she thought Estelle was being naive. "I know that. You know that. But my father did something far worse. He betrayed not only my mother but the entire family. He betrayed everything we'd built our lives upon."

Is that why you killed him? Estelle wanted to ask.

"Did he get remarried?" Estelle asked, playing the fool.

Penelope snorted and took a long drink of wine. If Estelle wasn't mistaken, she was pretty sure Penelope was quite drunk.

"He never had the time," Penelope said.

"Why is that?" Estelle searched Penelope's face for signs of pain but found only ruthlessness.

Penelope stuck her tongue into the side of her cheek. She no longer looked like a rich and beautiful older woman. Rather, she looked drunk and half crazy.

Estelle realized Penelope wasn't fully ready to talk about the shipwreck yet. She decided on another tactic.

"What about your siblings? Were they angry about your father's affair?" Estelle asked.

Penelope gulped more wine. "They were even angrier than me," she said with a cackle. "My older brother was the angriest. He was the one who figured out just how evil our father's plan was."

Estelle thought of Roland, learning about Chuck's affair and second family. She itched to take a drink of her own wine to calm her nerves but held herself back.

"What is the name of your older brother?" Estelle asked. She wanted everything to be on tape.

"Nathanial Albright," Penelope said automatically. "He discovered that my father was going to marry a woman from nothing. Can you believe that?"

"How awful," Estelle lied. She was so close now. How could she get Penelope to go all the way? "Who was this woman? Did you ever meet her?"

"Thank goodness, no," Penelope scoffed. "Our father tried to get us all to meet a few times, but we refused."

You broke your father's heart, Estelle thought then.

"She was much younger, I take it?"

"She wasn't so much older than me," Penelope remembered. She reached for the bottle of wine and refilled her glass. How many had she had so far? Estelle had lost count. Before she knew what was happening, Penelope tipped the bottle toward Estelle, demanding that she put more in Estelle's glass, too. Apparently, she hadn't noticed that Estelle had barely drunk anything.

Good, Estelle thought as Penelope filled her glass nearly to the brim. *She wants to pretend to be a good host. I'll let her.*

"Did he meet her in Manhattan?" Estelle asked.

Penelope glowered at Estelle for a split second. Estelle felt a rush of fear.

"I believe he met her in France," Penelope said, taking a breath. "She was half Russian, half French. They could hardly communicate. Well, maybe my father spoke a little French, but not a lot." She furrowed her brow. "He certainly wasn't a linguistical genius. That's for sure. But my father was all over the place. Constantly traveling. I'm sure he had countless other mistresses. What made this one so special? My mother was heartbroken. She didn't leave bed for weeks when she heard about her."

Suddenly, Penelope launched into a story about her mother and her sister, a story that had nothing to do with Estelle's plot. A few minutes passed. Estelle's thoughts scrambled. How could she guide Penelope back to the shipwreck? Back to Natasha and Vivian? Her phone continued to record; that was good. But she hadn't thought to ask Sam if there was a time limit on these things. What if it ran out?

"Why didn't your father marry this woman?" Estelle asked, trying to keep her voice easy and small.

Penelope snorted. "I thought you were here to interview me about my life, Estelle Coleman. Why do you want to know so much about Natasha Morceau?"

Estelle nearly had a heart attack. She looked down at her squiggly notes and at her phone and wondered if there was a way to get out of the apartment building if she needed to. Or would the doormen lock her in the lobby until Penelope had her arrested?

But I haven't done anything wrong. Not really. I've just listened to a lonely woman talk and talk.

Penelope continued to glare at Estelle. Estelle didn't know what to do. Her hands were clammy.

"I'm sorry," Estelle stuttered, fixing a smile across her face. "I'm just trying to get the whole picture. You know? I want to understand the entire background. The entire story of your life."

But suddenly, Penelope burst into laughter. Her stomach bounced, and she swung her head to and fro. Tears sprang from her eyes. "You should see your face," Penelope cried. "You look so scared! Like I'm going to eat you or something!" Penelope continued to bark with laughter. "Come on, Estelle. I'm just teasing you."

Estelle thought she was going to collapse. She'd really thought it was over, then. But Penelope was playing with her like a cat to a mouse. She joined Penelope in her laughter and smacked her knee a few times. *I don't know if I can keep doing this,* she thought. *I'm in over my head.*

But then Penelope continued. "My father didn't ever marry that horrible home-wrecker Natasha because he died." She said it easily as though she were talking about the weather.

"I'm sorry to hear that," Estelle said.

"He drowned, actually," Penelope offered without Estelle prying. "Maybe you read about the shipwreck? It was off the coast of one of those islands. One of the ones you always write about in your books." She raised her eyebrows. "I don't know. My family never vacationed there. We always went to Europe or the Caribbean. Maybe it was Nantucket?"

It was Martha's Vineyard, but Estelle did not tell her. She feigned ignorance and shock. "A shipwreck?"

Penelope barked with laughter. "Doesn't it sound horrible? It sounds like something from an old book. Like he went out whaling and never came home. But he was on his multimillion-dollar cruise liner, sailing off for Puerto Rico with his new love and her daughter. Before he left Manhattan, he told his lawyer he wanted to remove me and my brothers and sisters from the will, if you can believe that. Obviously, he wanted my mother removed, as well. But us? His only children? It was heinous."

Estelle let her jaw hang open. Here we go.

"She had a daughter?" Estelle asked.

Penelope's eyes shone. "That horrible woman tried to sue our family for rights to the inheritance," she said. "She said that her daughter was our sister, that she and my father had been having an affair for years and years. Obviously, the lawsuit was thrown out like that." She snapped her fingers. "Our father was at the bottom of the ocean! There was no way to prove it—unless we agreed to a DNA test, which we most certainly refused to. We wouldn't give Natasha the time of day."

Estelle felt all the blood drain from her head. "Was there any chance it was true?"

Penelope raised her shoulders. "Who cares? My father was a horrible man. He got what he deserved. And Natasha and her rug rat got what they deserved, too. I'm sure they're still broke and alone somewhere, demonizing my family for what we 'did to them.'" Penelope used air quotes.

Actually, Vivian is nonverbal, and Natasha is nowhere to be found, Estelle did not tell her.

How could she get her to admit to causing the shipwreck?

"Did many people die in the shipwreck?" Estelle asked delicately.

Penelope nodded. "It was a stormy night. I'm told it was like something from a bad movie. The ship went up and over the waves as much as it could before it fell to pieces, apparently. You couldn't get me on another ship for years after that. Planes are fine; I can knock myself out with pills for a few hours. But a ship? A sailboat? All that time over the black ocean? No thanks."

Estelle grimaced. She noticed that Penelope's wine was nearly empty again. Was Penelope aware of what she said at this point? Or had she drunk so much that she would blabber about anything? Just in case, Estelle grabbed the bottle and topped Penelope off. Penelope's smile was loose and big.

"What did your siblings think?" Estelle asked. Maybe one of them had confessed? Perhaps Estelle needed to interview each of them?

Maybe this investigation was going to take longer than she'd planned.

"My siblings?" Penelope cackled. "Well, let's just say some of us were more shocked than others."

Ding, ding, ding! Estelle thought.

"What do you mean?" Estelle asked, playing dumb.

"How do I put this?" Penelope tilted her head back and opened her lips. "You said you wanted the entire picture of my life. Nothing held back?"

"It's for the good of the book," Estelle reminded her.

"It's fiction," Penelope said in a harsh whisper. "Right?"

"I'm a fiction writer," Estelle said. It wasn't a lie.

"I feel safe around fiction writers," Penelope said. "But my life is stranger than fiction."

Estelle leaned toward her. She wanted to urge her along. She wanted a confession.

"We were friendly with the captain of the cruise ship," Penelope said then, her eyes illuminated.

Thirty seconds passed. Penelope wagged her eyebrows as though hoping Estelle would get her hint. But Estelle needed a verbal confession.

Penelope added softly, "We'd known him for years. We knew he could be bought."

"Did the captain survive the shipwreck?" Estelle asked.

"He did," Penelope offered. "But let's just say he knew what was coming."

Estelle's lips formed a big round O. Under her breath, she asked, "How could he have staged something like that?"

Penelope's eyes were sharp crystals. Suddenly, they dropped down to Estelle's cell phone. In a harsh voice, she demanded, "Are you recording?"

Estelle felt as though she'd been smacked. Fear pressed against her chest. Could she lie?

"I always record my interviews," Estelle stuttered. "I never show them to anyone."

But Penelope's face had lost its drunken sloppiness. She was on her feet, towering over Estelle in her stilettos. Estelle was suddenly very aware of how far off the ground she was.

"I'll turn it off," Estelle said hurriedly, reaching for her phone to stop the recording.

Penelope extended her fingers. She wanted the phone. Estelle gaped at her. She had no plans to hand it over. Was Penelope really going to insist?

They remained like that for nearly a minute—Estelle

on the sofa and Penelope towering over her. She still hadn't offered a concrete confession; she'd only hinted at her and her siblings' involvement in the shipwreck. She'd hinted that the captain knew the accident was coming.

But suddenly, Penelope burst into laughter again. It was ominous and clown-like, and it made Estelle's blood run cold.

"Look at us!" Penelope said, smacking her palms on her thighs. "I can't believe I still get so upset over my father's stupid bastard child. She's probably dead in a ditch somewhere. And look at me here? Look at everything I have. I basically run this city. I'm the legitimate daughter of Roger Albright. I'm his legacy. Everything I touch turns to gold."

Estelle laughed nervously and shoved her phone into her purse. She hadn't gotten that last part on the record, but, to her, it was Penelope's confirmation that Vivian was their little sister. Vivian was a real Albright.

Maybe there was another way to confirm that the children had paid the captain to sink the boat. Perhaps the "confession" she'd recorded was already enough?

Estelle rerouted their interview back to the subject of Penelope Albright and her "glittering successes." Penelope was pleased to chat more about her own brilliance. Estelle took more gibberish notes and even drank half a glass of wine to calm her nerves. She told herself to stay just another thirty minutes—enough time for Penelope to forget about their jagged exchange.

After that, Estelle thanked Penelope for her time, shook her hand, and promised she'd send her the book "first thing" when it was finished.

"I need a final say on everything," Penelope said in singsong as she walked to the elevator. "My name and my legacy mean everything to me." She pressed the button for the lift and touched Estelle's shoulder. Her smile was sinister and beautiful, showing too many of her very white teeth. "Just remember, Estelle Coleman. My lawyers are the most powerful in Manhattan and, therefore, the most powerful in the world. If you try to mess with me, I'll flatten you like a pancake."

Estelle felt her heart drop into her stomach.

The elevator doors opened. The elevator operator bowed and said, "Good evening, Ms. Albright."

Was it already evening? Estelle had lost track of time. She met Penelope's gaze a final time and stepped into the elevator.

"Thanks again," Estelle said in a shaky voice.

"Ta-ta!" Penelope said as the doors closed between them.

Estelle thought she was going to faint.

"She's a fabulous woman, isn't she?" the elevator operator clucked.

"She's one of a kind," Estelle breathed. "That's for sure."

But what was she going to do about it?

Was Estelle really brave enough to take her and the rest of the Albrights down—for the sake of Vivian and Natasha?

Was it even possible?

Chapter Eighteen

Christmas Eve 1982

It was hard to believe it was two months since the shipwreck of the cruise liner *La Boheme*. From where he sat in the living room of his house with Mia and the girls, all lit up by the Christmas tree lights with a mug of eggnog in his hand, the memory of the thrashing ocean and the cold and angry storm felt decades away. Oriana and Meghan wore their Christmas pajamas —a new tradition Mia had decided upon—and they were cozied up on the other sofa, reading quietly. Mia was at the record player, flipping over the Bing Crosby record. Chuck took a long sip of eggnog and reminded himself of how far he'd come. *I'm happy. We're all happy.*

That was when he spotted the shadow in the backyard.

Chuck shot to his feet. Oriana and Meghan eyed him nervously. Oriana closed her book and said, "Dad, what's wrong?"

Chuck didn't want to alarm the girls. But he was

pretty sure the shadow he'd seen was moving. Was it a person? An intruder? Everyone knew that Christmas was a perfect time to steal. There were unopened gifts beneath the tree, and everyone was feeling especially cozy and off their guard.

Mia watched him like a cat. "What is it, Chuck?"

"I'm going to get another mug of eggnog," he said, steadying himself and smiling. "Does anyone want anything?"

"Maybe a cookie," Meghan said. She wasn't aware of any tension in the room and returned her attention to her book.

Chuck's heart swelled with love. He had to protect his family. No matter what this was.

Chuck hurried through the kitchen and into the mudroom, where he donned his coat and his boots. From the living room came the sound of Bing Crosby. Mia was telling the girls that it was nearly time to get ready for bed. "Santa will be here any minute." Chuck wasn't clear on whether Oriana still believed, but Meghan sure did. She'd written four letters to Santa in the past few weeks, her handwriting sloppy but eager.

Chuck walked out the back door and onto the porch. It was the first time he'd stepped out back after dark since October. He'd paid attention to Mia's rules. He'd been home for his family.

Now, he was home to protect them.

A man stood in the middle of the backyard. He was all bundled up, his eyes glinting with the light from their Christmas tree, his hands in his pockets. He swayed to and fro as though he were very drunk. Chuck struck out through the snow with his chin raised. He was angry. So angry that this man had decided it was okay to stand in his yard and leer at their window.

That was when he realized who it was.

"Clarence?" Chuck's hands were in fists at his sides. He was just three feet away. But he was right. Clarence was very drunk. Chuck could have knocked him over easily.

Clarence's eyes were difficult to read. He was more grizzled than he'd been two months ago, as though he'd spent the better part of the past two weeks drinking at that dive bar and picking fights. Who was taking care of the light? Was it still Travis? That poor kid.

Travis needed love. He needed compassion.

Abstractly, Chuck wondered if Clarence was drinking himself to death because he felt so guilty about the shipwreck. But Chuck had thought about that night over and over again. He'd come to the same conclusion. Chuck had seen it as soon as any of them could have. Lives would have been lost regardless—even if Clarence and Travis had been vigilant, even if Clarence hadn't been smoking outside.

Accidents happened out on the water all the time. That was the nature of man versus the wilderness.

Chuck hadn't returned to reading *Moby Dick*, maybe because it felt too close to home. Or perhaps it was because he felt so unfocused, out of his mind, and worried about his life and his mistakes.

There was so much he couldn't take back.

Chuck took a step toward Clarence. He squashed his instinct to touch the man's shoulder and tell him everything would be okay. He didn't know Clarence's life. He didn't know his heart.

"Clarence," Chuck said quietly, "are you all right?"

Clarence coughed into his hand. It was a horrible cough, one that spoke of a deeply engrained illness.

Chuck considered demanding that Clarence get off his lawn.

But how could he throw this sick and lonely man off his property on Christmas Eve?

"Clarence, can I get you a warm drink inside?" Chuck asked quietly. "Tea? Coffee?"

Clarence coughed and nodded.

Chuck led Clarence in through the side door. As Clarence removed his boots, Chuck hurried to the living room to ask Mia to take the girls upstairs.

"It's Clarence," he told her.

She looked like a spooked cat. Wordless, she hurried to gather the girls and guide them upstairs.

Chuck returned to the kitchen to find Clarence in his socks, staring out the back window at the black ocean.

"Is Travis watching the light?" Chuck asked as he put the kettle on.

"Travis ran off," Clarence said.

Chuck's heart dropped. "Do you know where he went?"

Clarence shook his head. Devastation was etched into the corners of his eyes.

Chuck considered asking about the lighthouse. Who would have been watching it if Clarence hadn't been there? But Clarence answered that, too.

"I quit the light," Clarence said. "I'm headed off the island. Tomorrow, if I can make it."

"Do you have somewhere to go?" Chuck asked.

Clarence shook his head. The kettle was boiling, and Chuck hurried to take it off the heat and pour it into a mug.

"Did you drive here?" Chuck asked.

"I walked from the light," Clarence explained.

Chuck pressed the hot mug into Clarence's hands. Clarence's face calmed. He stared down at the liquid as hot steam rolled over his cheeks.

Chuck could see the younger, handsome man that Clarence had once been, just for a moment. And then it was gone.

"I wish you'd never come here," Clarence said into the mug.

Chuck's heartbeat quickened. He didn't know what to say.

"She was the only woman I ever really loved, you know?" Clarence said. He took a small sip of hot tea and grimaced. "She was the only one who gave me any hope for myself."

Chuck knew better than to think Clarence was talking about Travis's mother. Clarence had already mentioned Mia at the dive bar. This was all about Mia, somehow.

He remembered Mia's reaction when he'd mentioned the lighthouse keeper for the first time. It had been as though she'd seen a ghost.

"But I get it," Clarence said. "You want to raise your girls. You don't want to miss the good times."

Chuck didn't know what to say. His throat was tight.

Suddenly, Mia appeared in the doorway between the living room and kitchen. She wore her thick, fluffy robe tied tight, and her hair was loose and pretty to her shoulders. Her eyes were on Clarence. It was clear she knew him down to her bones. It was also clear she didn't want him in her house with her girls and her new husband.

"Clarence," she said tenderly. "I need you to go."

169

Clarence's shoulders slumped. He took a long sip of tea and nodded.

A moment of silence passed. Mia didn't look at Chuck once. After that, she turned and went back upstairs to take care of the girls.

Chuck looked around the kitchen—at the artwork on the fridge, at the Christmas cookies on the counter, and the Christmas cards that littered the table. He was grateful for all of it. He also knew it could be taken away at any second.

Life was precious and breakable.

Clarence sat down at the table and finished his tea. It was clear he didn't want to talk.

When he was finished, Chuck said, "I'll drive you home."

Clarence nodded.

In the truck, Chuck wondered what Clarence had come here for. Had he come to see Mia a final time? To say goodbye? Or had he just wanted to see Mia in her "real" environment—with her children by the Christmas tree? Had he wanted to torture himself?

Clarence was slightly more sober than he'd been and able to direct Chuck back to his cabin. Chuck kept the engine running and watched Clarence get out. But before he closed the door, he reached in and shook Chuck's hand.

"Be well, Chuck," he said. "Be grateful for what you have."

Chuck nodded and watched Clarence mill drunkenly through the snow and back into his cabin. His head throbbed.

He wanted to drive back home and crawl into bed with Mia. He wanted to wake up tomorrow and watch his daughters open their presents. He didn't want to think about Roland, Grant, and Margaret on Nantucket— spending Christmas together, their first without him.

But when Chuck was driving back home, he realized the island was blacker than ever. It felt like the harshest of nights.

It took a minute for him to realize why.

The lighthouse was dark.

He remembered what Clarence had said. He'd quit. But had he quit only in his mind? Left the lighthouse and walked down to Chuck's and Mia's. Maybe.

Chuck drove to the lighthouse and parked. The door at the base was wide open as though Clarence hadn't bothered to close it behind him. Chuck bounded inside and up and up and up to the top, where he performed all the rituals he'd watched Travis and Clarence do. Within a few minutes, miraculously, he had the light back on.

The little room at the top of the tower was a mess. Empty whiskey bottles and cans of beer were everywhere. It stank of a man at the end of his rope. Slowly, Chuck cleaned up, putting bottles into trash bags and wiping countertops. He wondered how quickly they would be able to hire a new lighthouse keeper. Was that a job people wanted to do anymore? It sounded romantic, but the reality was far different.

Maybe Chuck could step in for a while.

But not forever. The darkness felt too sinister. He wanted to be home.

Chuck managed to stay awake all night to tend to the light. He watched the stars and thought about his childhood when he'd believed in Santa Claus and magic. Now, he was fifty-one years old. What was headed toward him next? How long would he be alive?

Would Mia outlive him? Would he ever see Nantucket again?

When morning came, Chuck left the lighthouse and drove to the police station to report the problem. Everyone at the station was wearing Santa hats and eating cinnamon rolls. They threw their arms around him and thanked him for taking over the light.

"We're glad to have you over on our side of the sound, Chuck Coleman," one of them said.

"Glad to be here," Chuck said. "Let me know if you need anything at all."

As Chuck drove home, he felt grounded on Martha's Vineyard for the first time. It was his new home.

Back at home, Oriana and Meghan were already up and eager to open presents. They couldn't stop jumping around. Mia looked tired but beautiful, like she'd waited up all night, thinking of Clarence and Chuck. Chuck had wanted to call her, but the lighthouse had only a walkie-talkie. Now, she threw her arms around Chuck and whispered into his ear, "I love you."

Chuck wasn't sure what had happened. But he knew he had to bide his time. Maybe she'd tell him the truth eventually.

Perhaps he even deserved the truth this time.

It wasn't till that evening that Mia sat him down and explained. Oriana and Meghan were watching a Christmas movie on the sofa, tuckered out and over-sugared. Mia and Chuck were in the kitchen, talking in low voices.

Mia took a breath. *Here it comes*, Chuck thought.

"It was when Oriana was five and Meghan was two," Mia said. "You hadn't been back to Martha's Vineyard in more than five months. You were traveling for business, and Margaret had a health scare. And I was pretty sure you would never move here. I was sure you'd never be with me.

"I'd always known Clarence. We grew up together. But I ran into him near the lighthouse during a walk with the girls. I asked him for help with something at home. A little task, maybe to fix something, and he stayed for dinner. He was having trouble with Travis, and I gave him some advice. One thing led to another."

Mia's hands were shaking. Chuck took both of them and kissed her palms.

"I ended it six months later," Mia said. "I only loved you. He obviously didn't take it well. But I only wanted you. I was just so lonely."

Chuck's heart cracked. But he had to listen. He had to understand how it had been for Mia.

He'd left her here; he'd expected her to care for their daughters by herself. She'd needed a companion. She'd needed to feel loved.

"But you're here now," Mia breathed. "I know that."

Chuck bowed his head. He thought back to that night in October when the ship had sunk. He remembered she'd left the following evening. Where had she gone? Was he allowed to ask?

It was as though Mia could read his mind. "I had to ask him to leave you alone," Mia breathed. "I wanted to protect you from what I'd done. But I understand that if we're going to be married—if we're going to make this work—we have to be honest with each other. We have to put all our cards on the table."

Chuck filled his lungs. "All my cards are on the table. You know everything."

Mia raised her shoulders. "You know everything, too."

173

Chuck tried to laugh, but it sounded all wrong. "What do we do now?"

Mia was quiet for a moment. "Maybe we make eggnog and sit by the fire? Perhaps we raise our girls? Maybe we live the rest of our lives in peace and love?"

Chuck's eyes filled with tears. He wanted to put the past to rest. He sought to move on.

"It sounds like a plan to me," he said.

Chapter Nineteen

Present Day

It was Christmas Eve on Nantucket Island. Estelle was in her office, watching snow flutter down outside, listening as Roland struggled to wrap the rest of his presents down the hall. Perhaps he'd never mastered the art because he didn't have a creative bone in his body. It meant that his presents to Estelle were always crookedly wrapped and clumsy. Estelle didn't mind. She equated messiness with love. Plus, Roland was a perfectionist in so many other capacities. It was nice to find a few flaws.

Estelle was finishing up some notes for her actual romance novel—the one about the lighthouse keeper. Obviously, she didn't include anything about the Albright family in her notes. But she had decided to include a sinking ship and a lost inheritance—purely because it was all too good, story-wise, to pass up.

She was a writer, after all. She couldn't resist.

But ever since Estelle's trip to Manhattan, she hadn't

been able to get Penelope Albright and her near-confession out of her mind. As soon as she'd returned from that wild, exhilarating, and terrifying trip to New York, Estelle had reached out to her lawyer and told him her suspicions. She'd sent the file of her interview, too.

Now, her lawyer sent an email that read:

Dear Estelle,

I wanted to reach out to you regarding your suspicions about the Albright family and the sinking of *La Boheme* back in 1982. It's a tricky situation and not one that I take lightly. After listening to the recording of your interview with Penelope Albright, I share your belief. The Albright children almost certainly had something to do with their father's death. More than that, they're well-versed in hiding it.

After doing a bit of digging, I found that Natasha Morceau fought twice more to have her daughter recognized as an heir to Roger Albright's fortune. Each time, she was essentially laughed out of court.

It isn't right.

But as your friend, I want to say this clearly. I do not recommend that you go to war with these people. They have incredibly powerful lawyers. They've thrown millions of dollars into hiding what they've done and are not afraid to throw more.

They've killed, and they aren't afraid to kill again to protect their reputation.

Please, Estelle. Take a step back.

There are things in this world we cannot change.

I'm terribly sorry about that.

But I also looked into your other question—the one regarding the whereabouts of Travis Knight. I'm sorry to pass along more bad news.

Unfortunately, Travis Knight died earlier this year in a tragic car accident. He was living in Hyannis at the time, which may be why his wife was taken to the retirement facility nearby in Martha's Vineyard. I spoke with a woman at the police station in Hyannis. She said that shortly after Travis's accident, Vivian Knight plunged into darkness and stopped speaking. Prior to that, she lived a vibrant life; she was very involved in her community, and she loved Travis dearly. Despite being raised in France, she was a New Englander in every respect.

Vivian and Travis never had any children. She has no family nearby.

Her last remaining relative is her mother, Natasha. She's located in Paris. I can give you her contact details if you like. Coincidentally, I'm friendly with her lawyer.

I'm terribly sorry, but I can't help you more with the Albright family.

As always, I look forward to your next book.

Merry Christmas to you and yours,

Sheldon Martin

Estelle reread her lawyer's email with tears in her eyes. Before she knew what she was doing, she was on her feet, running down the hall to burrow herself in her husband's arms. Roland knew exactly what she needed. He held her as she cried and cried. When she was ready to talk, he listened as she spilled the entire story—explaining the lengths she'd gone to try to "make things right" for Vivian.

Roland didn't speak until she was done.

It was an incredible story—one from 1982, the time after his father had gone.

Estelle prayed it wouldn't upset him too much.

"You want her to have her inheritance?" Roland asked.

"I want her to have what's rightly hers," Estelle said. "I want her to be acknowledged by this evil family. And I want them to acknowledge what they did to Roger! I want them to pay!"

Roland shook his head ever so slightly. He took both of her hands in his. "We will help her with whatever she needs," he said instead, his words quiet. "If it's money she needs, we'll give her that. If it's care and friendship and love—we'll give her that in spades."

Estelle took a breath. Compassion echoed from her husband's eyes.

All this time, she'd been looking for a valid ending to a complicated story. She'd been looking for justice. But the world wasn't always a place where the good guys won and the bad guys lost. It was complicated, filled with ups and downs and sorrows and small joys.

Maybe it was up to Estelle to offer a little more joy for Vivian.

Perhaps it was up to her to bring Natasha back.

Maybe a mother's love was all Vivian really needed—especially so soon after her husband's death.

"I love you, Roland," she said, pressing her face into his chest. She didn't know what she'd do without him.

Later that evening, Oriana and Reese brought Chuck over for Christmas Eve dinner. Like Thanksgiving, Chuck planned to stay the night at Estelle and Roland's. This time, Estelle hugged him extra long. He'd let her into his complicated past. He'd let her see him.

In front of the crackling fire, Estelle explained what she'd done—that she'd gone to Manhattan to talk to an Albright, that her lawyer had told her to back off.

"And I learned that Travis is gone," she said quietly. "He died earlier this year. That's what sent Vivian spiraling. My suspicion is that it's related to hitting her head during the accident in 1982, but who knows?"

"The brain is a complicated thing," he agreed somberly. His eyes were to the fire.

They listened quietly as Roland, Grant, Katrina, Oriana, and Meghan laughed about something in the kitchen.

Estelle still wondered what it was about that night in 1982 that had changed Chuck's life. Would he ever tell her? Or would he keep that secret forever?

"I'm going to France in January," Estelle said suddenly. It was as though a light bulb went off in her head.

Chuck raised his eyebrows.

"Natasha lives there," Estelle said. The corners of her lips turned into a smile. "You think she'd be open to seeing me?" She paused. "Seeing us, I mean?"

Chuck laughed. "Don't you think I'm too old to travel that far?"

"Who says you're too old?" Estelle asked.

Chuck was contemplative. After a moment, he asked, "Do you think she knows about Vivian?"

"I don't," Estelle offered. "Otherwise, she'd be here, wouldn't she? She'd be by Vivian's side?"

Chuck nodded. "She hardly left her side after the accident."

"She only left to fight for her rights in court," Estelle remembered.

"She was a wonderful mother," Chuck said quietly.

"I can't imagine that love has changed in the slightest," Estelle said.

Chuck's face broke into a wide smile. "Let's do it," he said softly. "Let's go to Europe and find Natasha!"

Chuck and Estelle clasped hands. Estelle felt as though they were on a wild adventure together. Her heart felt open.

Even if she couldn't pin the blame on the Albrights, she was doing what she could to save Vivian and Natasha. It was all she had left.

Chapter Twenty

Chuck spent all of Christmas Eve and Christmas Day overwhelmed with love for his family. He enjoyed platter after platter of food. He drizzled too much gravy on his turkey, got extra helpings of cake and cookies and pie, and over-imbibed on wine. Eventually, he passed out upstairs at Roland's place, his stomach full and his head woozy. Miraculously, he woke up the day after Christmas feeling relatively all right.

More than anything, he was ready to get back home.

That morning before Roland took him to the ferry, still more snow fluttered down from a thick blanket of gray clouds. Estelle made a pot of coffee and offered cinnamon rolls, but Chuck declined anything sugary. "Just the coffee, thanks."

He would get something healthy when he got back to the retirement home. Oatmeal, maybe. Fruit.

He wanted to return to his routine. He was grateful for his routine.

But more than anything, he was grateful for the new addition to his routine—Sylvia.

He couldn't believe how quickly he'd fallen for her.

He dreaded telling his family about her. He was worried they'd say or think something like, *Aren't you too old to fall in love again?*

But Chuck's heart was working very, very well. It was the only thing that functioned just as it always had.

He'd tell them about Sylvia when he was ready. He wanted to make sure it stuck first. He felt as giddy as a teenager.

Over coffee that morning, Chuck and Estelle talked more about the specifics of their approaching trip to France. It was hard for Chuck to believe he'd leave the country at this age; hard to believe he'd sit on an airplane for seven or so hours; hard to believe he'd manage the time difference. But then again, why not? As long as his doctor cleared him, he was willing and able to go anywhere. Roland agreed to go, too.

"Maybe Rachelle can swing over to meet us," Estelle said excitedly. "Italy is just a country away."

Chuck beamed. It felt as though the plans were fully forming now.

But it was hard to imagine seeing Natasha again.

"When was the last time you saw her?" Estelle asked.

Chuck considered this. He tore through his memories —all the way back to November of 1982. It must have been around the time Vivian got out of the hospital. By then, it wasn't clear to any of them that Vivian and Travis would end up together. (Looking back, Chuck realized that Travis ran away in December of 1982 to chase Vivian.)

"She made some food for Mia and me and dropped it off right before Thanksgiving," Chuck remembered. "It was a French quiche. Absolutely sensational. She said she and Vivian were leaving the island, and they would never come back." His voice caught in his throat.

"Did you know she'd had that affair with Roger?" Estelle asked.

Chuck shook his head. "I was trying to stay out of other people's drama. I was trying to focus on my life." He bowed his head. He felt Roland's eyes on him. What was he thinking?

But when Chuck looked up to catch Roland's eye, he saw only compassion and curiosity.

Roland was now older than Chuck had been in 1982. *We're doing the best we can*, Chuck thought.

"I figured Natasha and Vivian went back to France together," Chuck said.

"I guess Travis apprehended them," Estelle said.

"It's romantic," Chuck offered.

"It's also tragic," Estelle said. "It divided mother and daughter for decades."

Until now, Chuck thought. He took a sip of coffee and gazed out the window. It looked as though the Nantucket Sound was frozen beneath a sparkling cerulean sky. But it was impossible for the entire ocean to turn to ice. He knew that.

Hours later, Chuck returned to the retirement facility. Sylvia was waiting for him in the living room of his suite, where she'd made tea and had little Christmas cookies sitting out. "My daughter made too many," she explained. She kissed him hello.

"If I ever see another Christmas cookie again, it'll be too soon," Chuck said with a happy laugh.

Sylvia groaned and clutched her stomach. "I know exactly what you mean!"

Chuck laughed and turned toward his Bluetooth

speaker to turn on Christmas songs. "I can't get enough of these, though."

"Silver Bells" played. His shoulders fell. Sylvia wrapped her arms around him and began to sway in time with the music. For the hundredth time since they'd reconnected a couple of weeks ago, they kissed with their eyes closed. Chuck felt as though he was floating.

He imagined Oriana saying, *Aren't you a little old for this, Dad?*

Of course, she would never say that. Chuck needed to stop worrying so much about what Oriana thought, anyway. She loved him. She wanted the best for him. That was that.

Sylvia and Chuck cozied up on his sofa with a film he'd never seen before. Ordinarily, he would have put on a history documentary and abandoned the world. But now, as dramatic stories unfurled on his television screen, Sylvia shifted uneasily and made soft comments about the characters. "Don't do that!" she begged. Chuck grinned.

They drank a small glass of wine an hour before bed. Chuck fought the urge to tell her he loved her. He certainly didn't, not yet. But maybe soon.

Instead, he said, "Let's go say good night to Vivian."

Sylvia smiled. "Let's do it."

They walked hand in hand through the halls of the retirement facility, headed for the television room, where Vivian always sat by herself. *Soon, she won't be alone,* Chuck told himself. But he prayed nothing would go wrong in Paris. What if Natasha was too sick to come back? What if she no longer cared about Vivian? What if she felt betrayed that Vivian had stayed behind to marry Travis rather than return to France with her?

Vivian was wrapped in a blanket and watching *It's a*

Wonderful Life. Chuck and Sylvia pulled up chairs on either side of her and watched for a while. They'd seen the movie what felt like hundreds of times. Somehow, it never got old.

The wine went to Chuck's head shortly thereafter. Soon, he was unable to stop himself. He touched her shoulder.

Vivian flinched and turned her head ever so slightly. He wondered if she could hear him—somewhere in there.

"My son and I are going to help you," he said softly. "We're going to help you with whatever you need."

Vivian's eyes glowed. It was difficult to know if she understood. He prayed she did.

Chapter Twenty One

It was the third week of January and the day before the big trip to France. Estelle had her suitcase open on the floor of her walk-in closet, mulling over her final outfit options, imagining herself in the scenes of the proceeding days—in the office of the international film production company, in the swanky apartment of Natasha Morceau, and sitting at a café with her love Roland, people-watching. She knew French women had an eye for design that they didn't hesitate to enjoy the finer things in life. Estelle wanted to fit in—if only for a moment—before she returned to Nantucket, where she belonged.

Hilary was on Estelle's bed, watching her and drinking from a mug of tea. Behind her was a stack of wedding magazines. But she hadn't opened them since she'd swung by to say good luck. Estelle knew that most of Hilary's wedding was already set. All Hilary had to do was sit back, relax, and wait for time to pass. But Estelle also knew that her youngest child wasn't her most patient one. She stepped out of the closet and touched Hilary's shoulder gently.

"Penny for your thoughts?" Estelle asked.

Hilary pressed her lips together. "I can't stop thinking about marriage."

Estelle cocked her head with surprise.

Hilary spread her palms across her thighs and gazed out the window. It was snowing again. It had been a spectacular year for it.

"All these stories you've dealt with lately," Hilary said. "They involve Grandpa Chuck and Grandma Margaret; his second wife, Mia; Roger Albright and his first wife and his mistress. It doesn't give me much hope for my marriage."

Estelle sat at the edge of the bed next to Hilary and took her hand. She studied her eyes, remembering that it wasn't so long ago they'd thought Hilary was going blind. It was a miracle she could still see.

"But Marc loves you, Hilary," Estelle said softly. "He loves you so much that he left his life out west for you. He wants to start a new chapter with you. It's a once-in-a-lifetime opportunity."

Hilary bowed her head. "What if it ends in disaster?"

Estelle placed her head on Hilary's shoulder. "There is always the possibility of disaster. But we love and live anyway."

She thought of the shipwreck of the La Boheme; she thought of the photograph she'd seen of its stern, sticking out of the sea.

Hilary carried Estelle's suitcase downstairs and put it in Roland's car truck. They hugged a final time, then drove off to the airport. Ordinarily, they took the ferry to the mainland and flew out of Boston, but Roland had arranged for a special private plane for the benefit of Chuck's comfort. It had been a long time since Estelle had flown on a private plane. She felt giddy and eager to stretch her legs and sleep somewhere over the ocean.

If I can sleep at all, she thought. I'm so nervous!

When they arrived, Chuck, Oriana, and Reese were waiting for them at the airport. Oriana and Reese had brought Chuck to Nantucket and then texted last night to say they wanted to swing over to Paris, too. "If there's room on the plane!"

Roland had told them the more, the merrier.

Estelle led the charge onto the private plane and set herself up next to Roland. Chuck was seated on the other side of the aisle. Like always, he was dressed to the nines in a pair of corduroy pants and a button-down, and his hair was styled with gel. There was a rumor going around that Chuck had a girlfriend at his retirement facility, but Estelle hadn't felt brave enough to ask the man himself. Oriana had heard the gossip, but she was too frightened to ask, too.

Everyone wanted to give Chuck Coleman space and time to heal—and write his next chapter. He was ninety-three, but he wasn't going anywhere any time soon.

The plane took off smoothly. Before Estelle knew it, they were far over the blue ocean, popping champagne and telling old stories. Estelle told a joke that made Oriana laugh so hard that champagne burst out of her mouth.

Oriana explained that she had several client meetings set up in Paris. "I haven't been in ages," she said dreamily. "But I can't wait to get my hands on a perfect baguette."

Reese rubbed his palms together happily.

"If only Rachelle could come," Chuck said, crossing his ankles.

"She's busy at the restaurant," Estelle said sadly. "Maybe we can make a last-minute pit stop in Rome. We have the private plane for a little while. Don't we, Roland?"

Roland beamed. "I've already asked the pilot if he's free."

Estelle and Chuck cheered with joy. Within the week, they'd be seated at a grand table at Rachelle's restaurant, eating to their hearts' content.

But right now, they had a job to do in Paris. Two jobs, actually.

The first was Estelle's meeting with the production company. To get it out of the way, Estelle decided to head immediately to the hotel, freshen up, and go to the production company offices. They welcomed her with a glass of champagne and a platter of fine fresh cheeses and cured meats.

"Bonjour, Madame Coleman!" This was Pierre, a man she'd spoken to via Zoom several times. His accent was even more pronounced offline. "We've been very much anticipating your arrival!"

Estelle beamed. "It's a dream come true to be here and chat about the film script. As you know, I wrote that book many years ago, but it's still close to my heart."

Pierre beamed and led her deeper into the production company, where she met investors and producers and, finally, the scriptwriter who'd taken the reins on her feature. The scriptwriter was a woman named Marion, with high cheekbones and luxurious chestnut-brown hair. Somehow, she reminded Estelle of Roland's Aunt Jessabelle, the feisty older woman they'd lost last year. Her heart banged with recognition.

For more than three hours, Estelle and Marion chatted about the script. Because Marion knew Estelle's book so well, talking to her felt like digging deeper into Estelle's own brain.

"I hope you'll find time to come back to France during filming?" Marion asked, smiling happily as they finished their meeting for the day.

"I plan on it," Estelle agreed. "But it might be difficult. I have a huge family back home. They count on me."

Marion tilted her head thoughtfully. "They count on you," she said, "but they also count on you to live your own life and become what you want to become. This is a great weight upon a woman's shoulder. She must carry her entire family, but she must carry her own dreams, too."

Estelle's heart swelled. "Well said."

She knew that Marion was the perfect woman to handle her story. She truly got her.

After she met with the production company, Estelle returned to the hotel to meet with Roland, Chuck, Oriana, and Reese. Oriana and Reese had spent all afternoon milling through the city while Roland and Chuck had taken the opportunity to rest. Chuck's coloring was healthy; his smile was infectious.

"I've taken it upon myself to make a reservation at an exclusive restaurant in the 5th," he announced, clapping his hands.

"Brilliant, Dad," Oriana said, swinging some shopping bags to and fro in her right hand. "I'll get ready right now!"

Estelle met Chuck's gaze that night at the restaurant over flickering candles. "Are you nervous?" she asked.

Chuck spread his palms out across the white linen tablecloth. A moment of secrecy passed between them. They were both so immersed in the story of Natasha and Vivian, the story of the sunken ship. Nobody else in their family could wrap their minds around it.

"I'm worried that seeing me will bring all that pain back to her," Chuck said, speaking of Natasha. "But I know that if we don't see her, she'll never see Vivian again."

Estelle hadn't said this aloud. But she had a private hope that Vivian would "wake up" from her darkness when she saw her mother again.

Maybe that was naive.

But Estelle was a romance writer. Perhaps that meant she would always be naive. Maybe that meant she was perpetually preparing herself for heartache—because she wanted too much from the world.

Natasha had agreed to receive Chuck and Estelle at three p.m. the following afternoon. That morning, feeling too jittery to do anything else, Estelle wandered the streets of Montmartre with Roland, taking funny photographs outside of the Sacre-Coeur and the old haunts of Toulouse-Lautrec. It was hard to believe Paris really existed. It looked more like a painting than a real place.

At three, she knocked on Chuck's hotel door. He answered it, already dressed and ready to go. "I was thinking we could take a cab," he said.

The hotel receptionist called a taxi service to pick up Estelle and Chuck. Roland walked them out and saw them off, telling them to call if they needed anything.

Estelle squeezed Roland's hand a final time and said, "I love you." Roland closed the door between them and watched them drive off.

Chuck and Estelle were wordless all the way to Natasha's apartment. It was as though the past had crept up and sat with them in the taxi. It was too heavy.

Just like Penelope Albright's apartment building in Manhattan, Natasha's had a doorman. But unlike Penelope Albright's apartment building, Natasha's didn't have some of the richest inhabitants in the entire city. They were upper-middle-class, older Parisians who'd worked hard and retired in their sixties. Through the lobby and up the elevator, they passed eight or nine residents. Estelle saw nobody under the age of forty-five.

Natasha lived on the fifth floor. The elevator dinged and let them out. When they turned down the hall, they saw a door open wide at the far end. In the doorway was a woman in her eighties—a gorgeous woman with a thick head of hair, thick eyebrows, and high cheekbones. Based on the fire in her eyes, Estelle knew already this was Natasha.

She was a woman who'd survived so much.

She was a woman who'd been wronged.

Chuck froze in the middle of the hall. Estelle studied his face and tried to imagine what he was thinking.

Maybe he was taken back to that stormy night in October 1982.

Natasha stepped forward. "Chuck?" Her voice was hesitant, and her accent was overwhelmingly French.

Estelle hoped her English was better than it had been in the past. Estelle and Chuck spoke no French, and she hadn't thought to bring a translator.

"Natasha," Chuck breathed. As quickly as he could,

he cleared the distance between them and took Natasha's hand. He gazed at her with shock.

A full minute passed before anyone said anything else.

"Please," Natasha said. "Come in." She hardly glanced at Estelle. But that was okay with Estelle. She was just along for the ride.

Natasha's apartment was small but beautifully decorated. Paintings hung on every wall; sculptures sat in corners; big, luscious plants filled the space. It took Estelle a little while to realize why the place gave her the creeps. It was because there were no photographs. Nothing indicated that Natasha had ever loved anyone or been loved. Estelle's stomach went cold.

Natasha led them into the living room, where she had a drink cart set up and offered them wine, tea, or juice.

"Nothing, Natasha," Chuck said quietly. "I don't want anything."

Natasha's eyes were liquid. She sat down across from him and reached over to take his hands. Estelle sat by Chuck and tried to make herself very small.

"After all these years, Chuck," Natasha breathed. "I cannot believe you are here with me."

Estelle breathed a sigh of relief. It was clear Natasha's English was better than it had been in the eighties.

"You look exactly the same," Chuck said.

Natasha cackled and threw her head back. "I'm an old woman, Chuck. When you met me, I was in my late thirties. I still had so much to give the world, and there was still so much the world wanted from me. But it is not so, now."

Chuck squeezed her hand harder. Estelle swallowed. Over the phone, Chuck had told Natasha only that he had something to talk to her about. He hadn't mentioned Vivian's name at all.

"When did you come back to France?" Chuck asked. He'd told Estelle he wanted to ease into it.

"I came back in eighty-three," Natasha said. "It was after three consecutive fights with the Albright lawyers. I couldn't take it anymore. The dream with Roger was over. He was dead; his money would never be my money. I needed to return to my home."

"It must have been a terrible time," Chuck said. "I'm sorry I wasn't there for you."

Natasha waved her hand. "You had young children and a wife at home. I'm sure you had much to deal with yourself."

Chuck bowed his head. His eyes stirred with memories.

"Your wife," Natasha said. "Is she still with us?"

"She's gone," Chuck said. "She died ten years ago."

Natasha sighed. "I am sorry to hear."

"Were you ever married?" Chuck asked.

Natasha shook her head. "I'm rather proud about that. I had relationships, of course. One of them lasted twelve years. But I always found a way to retain my independence. It was important to me, especially after what those Albrights did to me." She furrowed her brow.

"You really think they sank the boat?" Chuck asked.

"I am sure," Natasha said.

"Penelope Albright told me herself that the captain of the ship was paid handsomely," Estelle interjected. But immediately after she'd said it, she cursed herself. Why was she drudging up the past like this?

"I learned that myself," Natasha said. "The captain told me. He was dying of grief and guilt. But his confession did nothing for me. The Albrights were too power-ful." She bit her lower lip. "My daughter and I became estranged shortly after that. I had no will to keep fighting."

Estelle's heart seized.

"How did that happen?" Chuck asked.

Natasha puffed out her cheeks. "My daughter fell in love with an islander. She wanted to stay in America and marry him. I insisted that she come back with me. The man she wanted to marry had nothing. No money. No prospects. I couldn't understand it. But Vivian told me she had no interest in marrying for money. 'Not like you,' she said. That was harsh. I turned my back on her and went to the airport. After that, I didn't know where she was or what had become of her. I never knew if she really married that broke young man from Martha's Vineyard." She shuddered.

Estelle reached for her purse and pulled out the picture of Vivian and Travis—the same one she'd discovered in the Martha's Vineyard Historical Society. There was a lump in her throat. She handed it over.

Natasha took the photo. Her hands shook. "My beautiful daughter," she whispered. Her eyes filled with tears. "My darling girl."

A moment of silence passed. Estelle thought she was going to start sobbing.

But then Chuck took over. "Your daughter is back on Martha's Vineyard, Natasha."

Natasha's gaze returned to Chuck's. "I beg your pardon?" Her voice wavered.

"But she's not doing well, Natasha," Chuck said, palming the back of his neck. "She was checked into my retirement facility. She can't walk or speak."

Natasha's hands went to her mouth. Estelle thought the older woman was going to scream.

"They said this might happen," Natasha whispered. "They said the head injury was terrible. They said it could give her problems later in life. But I never imagined..." It seemed impossible for her to speak.

Chuck reached for Natasha's hand. "That's why I wanted to come find you, Natasha. Vivian has nobody. Her husband died earlier this year. She never had children. All she has left is her mother. And maybe her mother could bring her back to the world—if only just a little bit."

Natasha's shoulders shook. Tears spilled from her eyes.

But Estelle recognized Natasha's expression. It was one of purpose. She knew Natasha would board the plane with them back to the United States within the week (after a brief stopover in Rome, of course). She knew she would be by Vivian's side.

Motherhood is forever, Estelle thought. *Natasha's love is still necessary. It's still enough.*

Chapter Twenty Two

It was ten days later when the plane landed on Martha's Vineyard. Estelle gripped Roland's hand hard until the wheels stopped rolling and the side door opened to let them out. It was the beginning of February—a brand-new year—and even more snow had piled up on the islands, blanketing them in soft white.

Estelle watched Natasha gather her little backpack and put on a pair of thick sunglasses. Now that she wasn't in France anymore, her chicness was especially pronounced. Despite the long flight, she'd refused to wear anything but her finest clothing, while Estelle and Oriana had put on pajama pants and let themselves get comfy.

A little car came down the runway to pick up the guests on the private plane. From here, Roland planned to head to Reese and Oriana's place for dinner with Meghan and Hugo, while Chuck, Estelle, and Natasha went immediately to the retirement facility. Vivian was waiting for them.

Estelle hugged Roland extra tight as the taxi pulled up to the airport.

"You're a good person, Estelle Coleman," he breathed into her ear.

"I'm just chasing a story," she said, although she knew this was a lie. She'd given up on the "story" aspects of this a long time ago. She was dealing with real people.

She was reminded of her daughter, Sam. All day, every day, Sam worked to build better lives for the people of Nantucket Island. She met drug addicts, alcoholics and depressed people who said they couldn't go on, and she tried to convince them there was still so much to live for. It was an admirable pursuit, Estelle thought now. Maybe Estelle should try to do something like that more often. Maybe bringing Natasha and Vivian together was her first foray.

Natasha was pale during the drive to the retirement facility. When the car pulled up, she muttered in French and then turned to Chuck to say, "You tell me my daughter is living here? In this place for very old people?"

"For people like me," Chuck said.

Estelle got out and hurried around the car to let them out. She wanted to take Natasha's arm to make sure she got to the front door all right, but Natasha refused to have help. Chuck and Natasha walked side-by-side to the front door, which opened automatically and brought them into the warmth. Estelle shivered until she was deep inside the facility.

"Afternoon, Claire," Chuck said to an employee. "We're looking for Vivian. This is her mother."

Claire's eyebrows went to her hairline. She was genuinely shocked. "It's a pleasure to have you here!" she said. "Vivian is right this way."

Estelle thought she would throw up. She was terrified of what would happen next. Slowly, Claire led them to the living room with the television, directly to the same position where Vivian had sat day in and day out since her arrival.

The minute Natasha saw her for the first time, she froze. Her hands were in fists at her sides. She shook with tears.

Estelle couldn't imagine not seeing her children for forty years. She would never have let that happen.

But she couldn't blame Natasha for what had happened. Estelle had given up on being judgmental.

Natasha put a chair next to her daughter's wheelchair and took both of her hands. Chuck moved to turn off the television; nobody else was in the room, anyway.

Under her breath, in tender, motherly tones, Natasha spoke to Vivian in French. Her eyes filled with tears. But Vivian continued to stare straight ahead as though Natasha wasn't there at all.

Estelle suddenly realized that she didn't want to be here for this. She wanted to give them privacy.

Chuck followed Estelle into the living room next door. There, they stood in silence.

"It's still good they're together," Chuck whispered.

"They're all each other has," Estelle agreed.

Chuck looked weary. He sat down next to the fireplace and studied the fire.

From the next room, they could still hear Natasha speaking to Vivian in French. Could Vivian hear her? Did she understand anything?

"How is your book going?" Chuck asked at last.

"It's okay," Estelle said. "I've been distracted, to say the least."

"You have quite a lot of material to work with," Chuck said.

"I would never use something like this," Estelle said. "It's too private. Too sacred."

Chuck nodded. "I know what you mean."

Suddenly, a woman in her eighties entered the living area. She smiled at Estelle, but she was focused on Chuck. Chuck turned and looked at her. A blush crawled up his neck.

This is the woman he's falling in love with, Estelle realized.

"You're back," the woman said, dropping down to hug Chuck.

Chuck struggled to his feet and hugged the woman as tightly as he could. His eyes were closed.

Estelle thought it was a shame that so many "middle-aged" people considered older people "done" with life. It was so clear that older people wanted to live as much and as well as they could. Chuck wanted his heart to beat with love for a beautiful woman.

"How was France?" the woman asked.

"It was gorgeous," Chuck said. "And we even visited my great-granddaughter in Rome."

"You're a lucky man," the woman said.

"Maybe I can take you someday," Chuck said. He turned to look at Estelle. "But first, I'd like you to meet my son's wife. This is Estelle."

"I'm Sylvia," she said, reaching out to shake Estelle's hand.

"It's a pleasure," Estelle said.

Suddenly, from the next room came the sound of Natasha crying out. Estelle bolted toward the noise, frightened that something had happened. Maybe it was an emergency.

But she found Natasha back on her feet. Her eyes and

face were glowing with joy. "She heard me!" Natasha cried. She sounded sure of herself. "She squeezed my hand back!"

Chuck and Sylvia were hot on Estelle's heels. Together, the three of them looked at Natasha and Vivian. It was true something was different about Vivian's eyes; something spoke of health and vitality and happiness.

She looked more awake than Estelle had ever seen her.

Natasha was firm in her belief. "I'm not going back to France," she said, reaching down to take Vivian's hand. "I won't leave until Vivian can walk on that plane with me. I won't leave till she's well enough to tell me she loves me back."

Natasha could sense her daughter's beating heart. She could feel a future for them both.

Estelle knew better than to think Natasha was making it all up.

A mother knows, Estelle thought. *We always know.*

Coming Next in the Coleman Series

Pre Order April Flowers

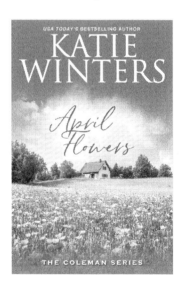

Other Books by Katie Winters

The Vineyard Sunset Series

Secrets of Mackinac Island Series

Sisters of Edgartown Series

A Katama Bay Series

A Mount Desert Island Series

A Nantucket Sunset Series

A Frosty Season Series

The Salt Sisters Series

The Sutton Book Club Series

Connect with Katie Winters

Amazon
BookBub
Facebook Newsletter

To receive exclusive updates from Katie Winters please
sign up to be on her Newsletter!
CLICK HERE TO SUBSCRIBE

Made in the USA
Columbia, SC
20 April 2025

56868931R00115